Dear parents, caregivers, and educators:

If you want to get your child excited about reading, you've come to the right place! Ready-to-Read *GRAPHICS* is the perfect launchpad for emerging graphic novel readers.

All Ready-to-Read *GRAPHICS* books include the following:

- ★ **A how-to guide to reading graphic novels for first-time readers**

- ★ **Easy-to-follow panels to support reading comprehension**

- ★ **Accessible vocabulary to build your child's reading confidence**

- ★ **Compelling stories that star your child's favorite characters**

- ★ **Fresh, engaging illustrations that provide context and promote visual literacy**

Wherever your child may be on their reading journey, Ready-to-Read *GRAPHICS* will make them giggle, gasp, and want to keep reading more.

Blast off on this starry adventure . . . a universe of graphic novel reading awaits!

Judge Kim and the Kids' Court

The Case of the Missing Bicycles

written by **Milo Stone, Shawn Martinbrough,** and **Joseph P. Illidge**

illustrated by **Christopher Jordan**

Ready-to-Read *GRAPHICS*

Simon Spotlight

New York   London   Toronto   Sydney   New Delhi

SIMON SPOTLIGHT

An imprint of Simon & Schuster Children's Publishing Division
1230 Avenue of the Americas, New York, New York 10020
This Simon Spotlight edition August 2022
Text copyright © 2022 by Shawn Martinbrough, Milo Stone, and Joseph P. Illidge
Illustrations copyright © 2022 by Christopher Jordan
For information about special discounts for bulk purchases, please contact
Simon & Schuster Special Sales at 1-866-506-1949 or business@simonandschuster.com.
Manufactured in the United States of America 0722 LAK
2 4 6 8 10 9 7 5 3 1
Library of Congress Cataloging-in-Publication Data
Names: Stone, Milo, author. | Martinbrough, Shawn, author. | Illidge, Joseph, author. |
Jordan, Christopher (Illustrator), illustrator. Title: The case of the missing bicycles / written
by Milo Stone, Shawn Martinbrough, and Joseph P. Illidge ; illustrated by Chris Jordan.
Description: New York : Simon Spotlight, [2022] | Series: Judge Kim and the Kids' Court |
Summary: When bicycles go missing at Fairville Elementary School, it is up to nine-year-old
Kim Webster to listen to witnesses and evidence presented by her friends and settle the
case in her tree house court. Identifiers: LCCN 2021058819 (print) | LCCN 2021058820
(ebook) | ISBN 9781665919630 (paperback) | ISBN 9781665919647 (hardcover)
ISBN 9781665919654 (ebook) Subjects: CYAC: Graphic novels. | Courts—Fiction.
Stealing—Fiction. | Bicycles and bicycling—Fiction. | LCGFT: Graphic novels.
Classification: LCC PZ7.7.S755 Cas 2022 (print) | LCC PZ7.7.S755 (ebook)
DDC 741.5/973—dc23/eng/20220304
LC record available at https://lccn.loc.gov/2021058819
LC ebook record available at https://lccn.loc.gov/2021058820

Cast of Characters

Kim Webster

her little brother:
Miles Webster

their dog:
Digger

Miles' best friend:
Miguel

Kim's friends:
Ally, Simone, and Gabby

classmate:
Neil Strong

new kid at school:
Corey Boone

This is Kim. She's here to give you some tips on reading this book.

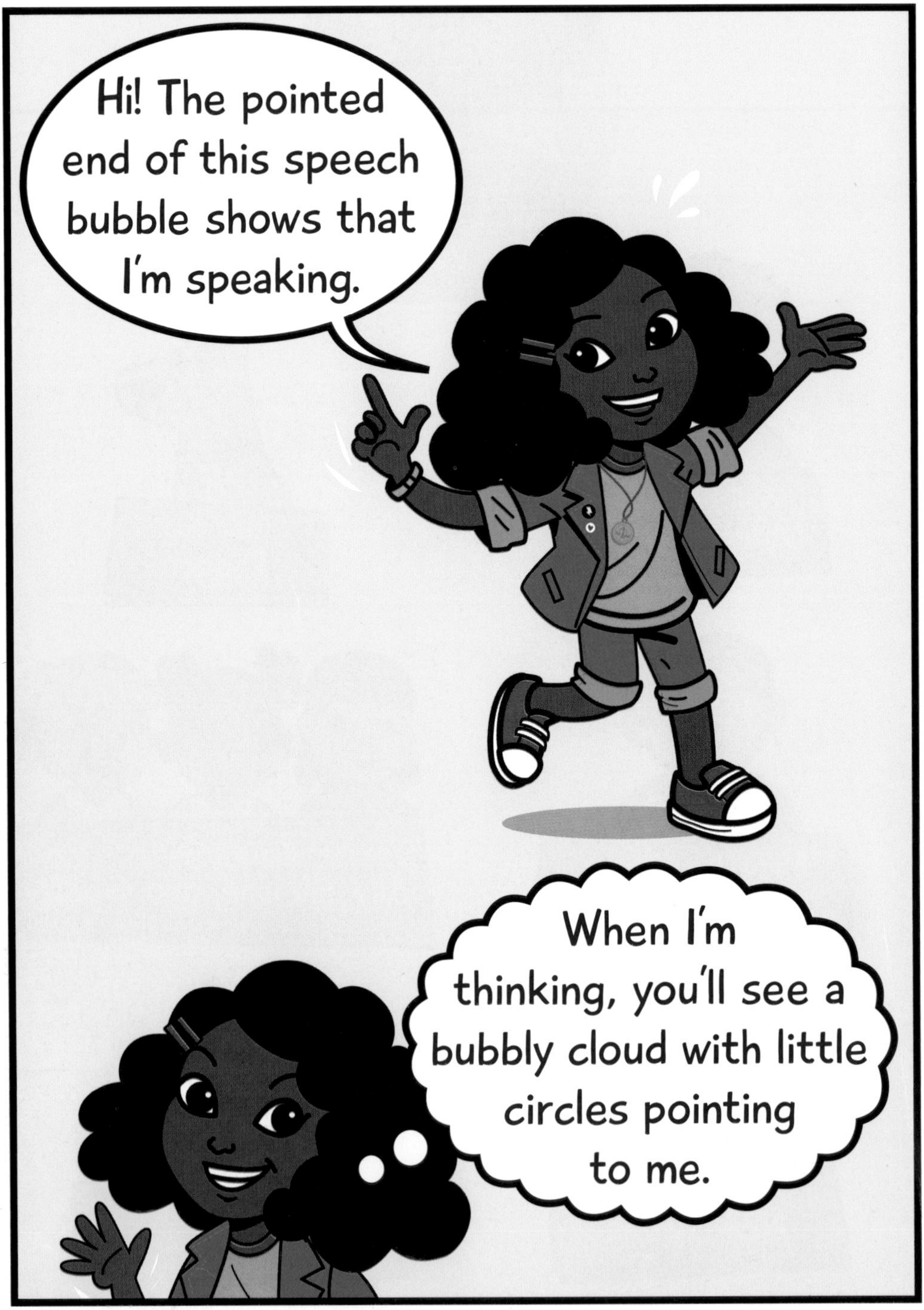
Hi! The pointed end of this speech bubble shows that I'm speaking.
When I'm thinking, you'll see a bubbly cloud with little circles pointing to me.

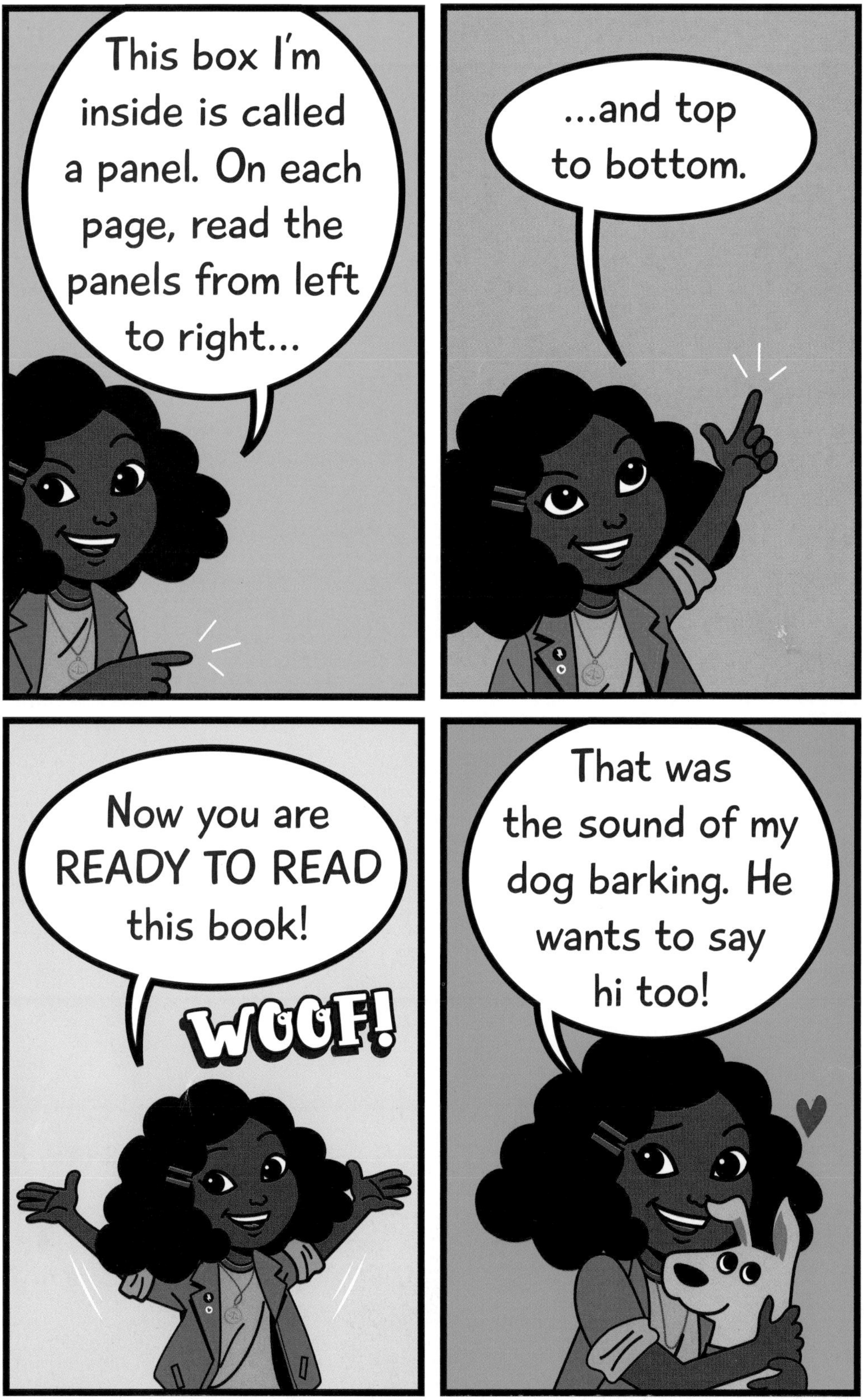
This box I'm inside is called a panel. On each page, read the panels from left to right...
...and top to bottom.
Now you are READY TO READ this book!
WOOF!
That was the sound of my dog barking. He wants to say hi too!

It's a beautiful morning in the town of Fairville.

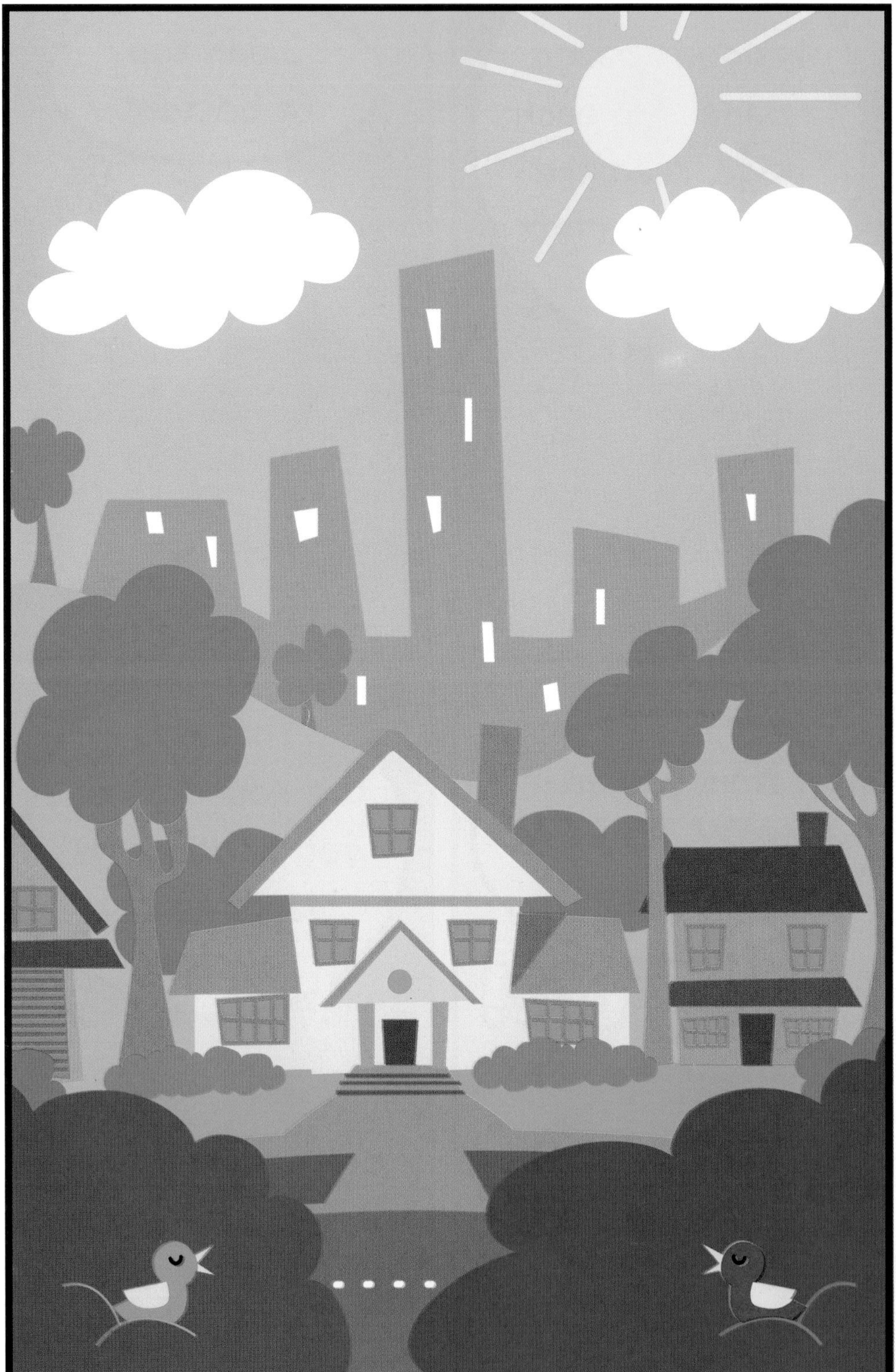

Kim Webster and her dog, Digger, are still sound asleep.

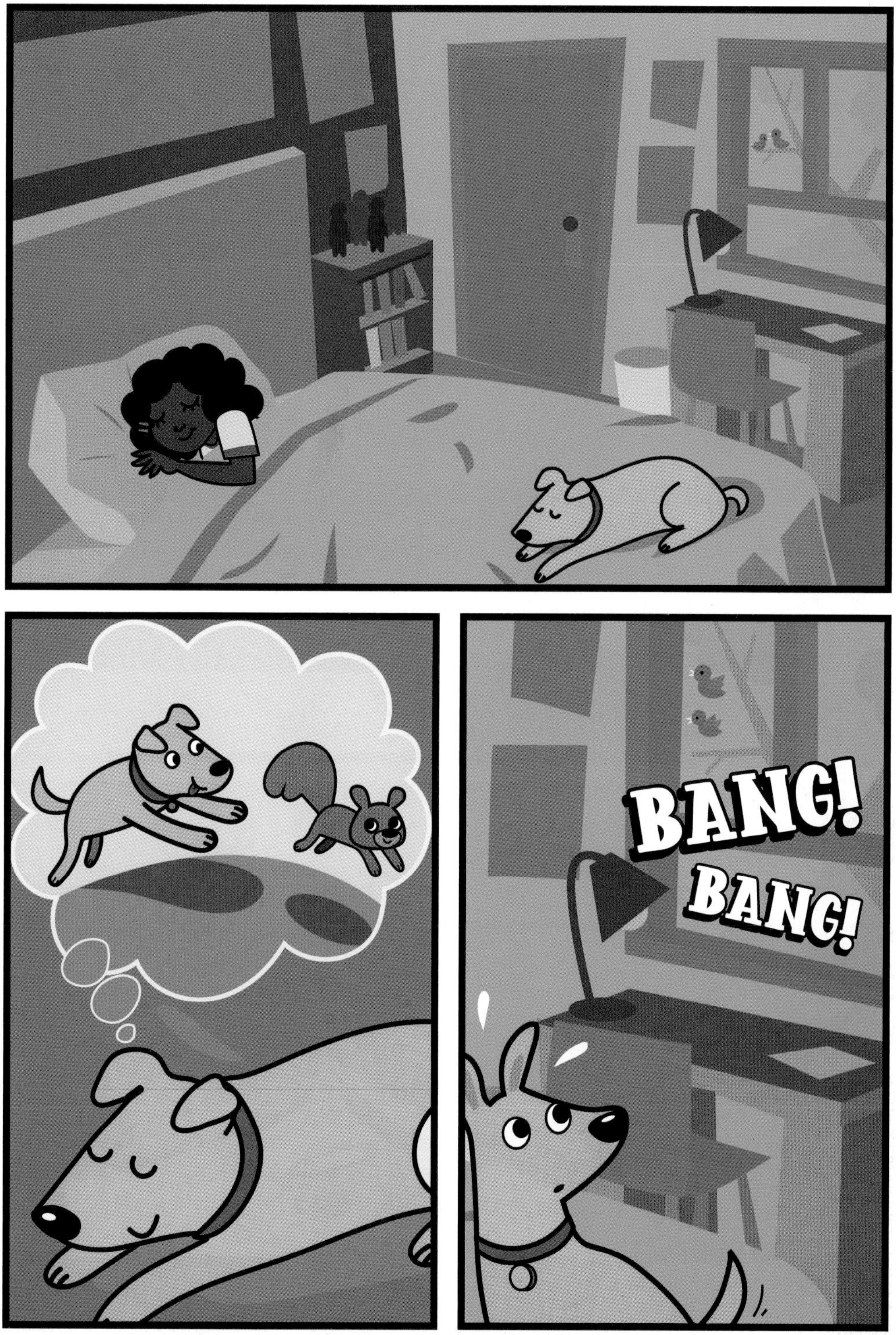
BANG!
BANG!

Sometimes Kim has trouble getting up for school...

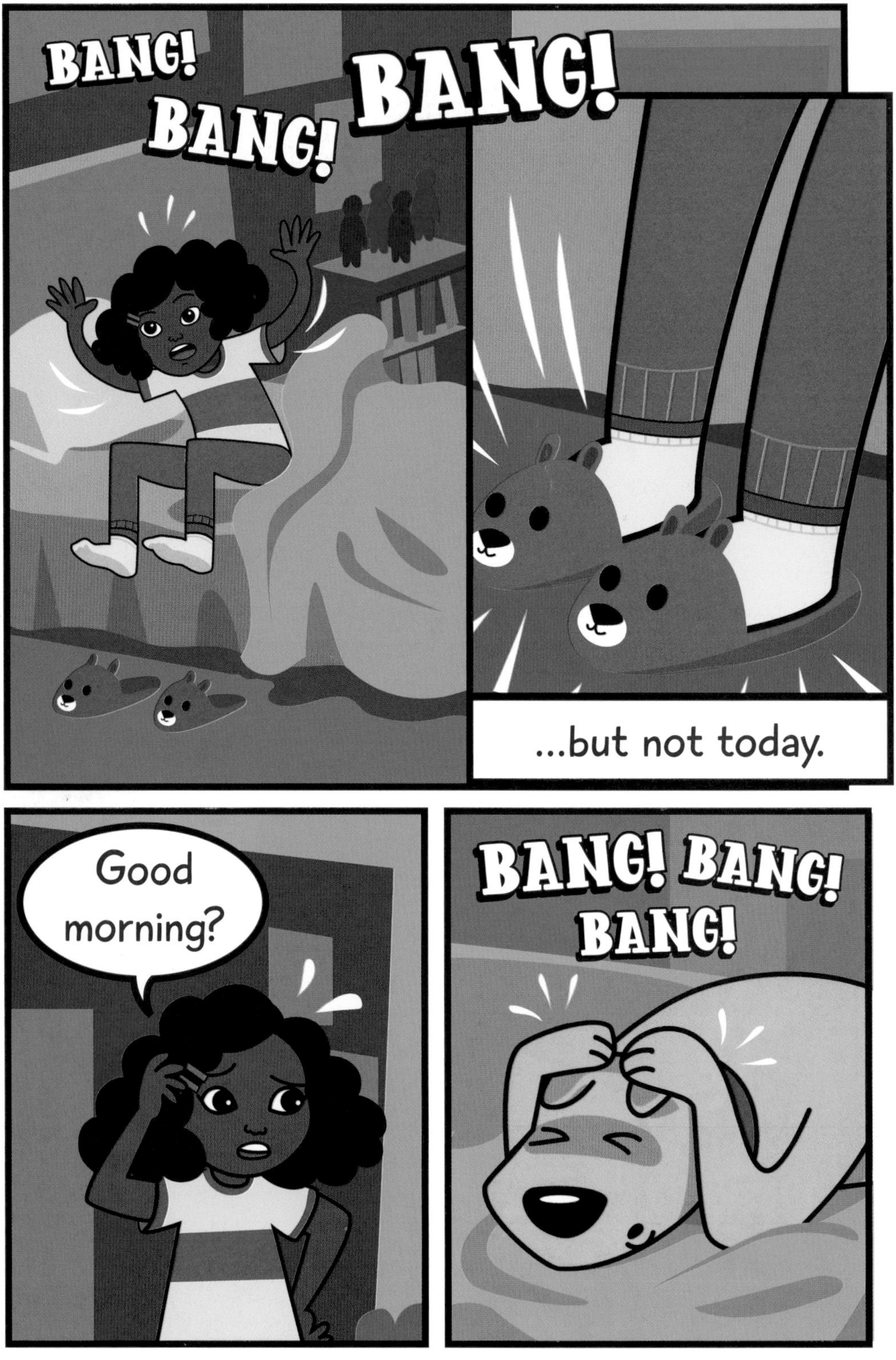
BANG!
BANG!
BANG!
...but not today.
Good morning?
BANG! BANG!
BANG!

Kim follows the noise that interrupted her slumber.

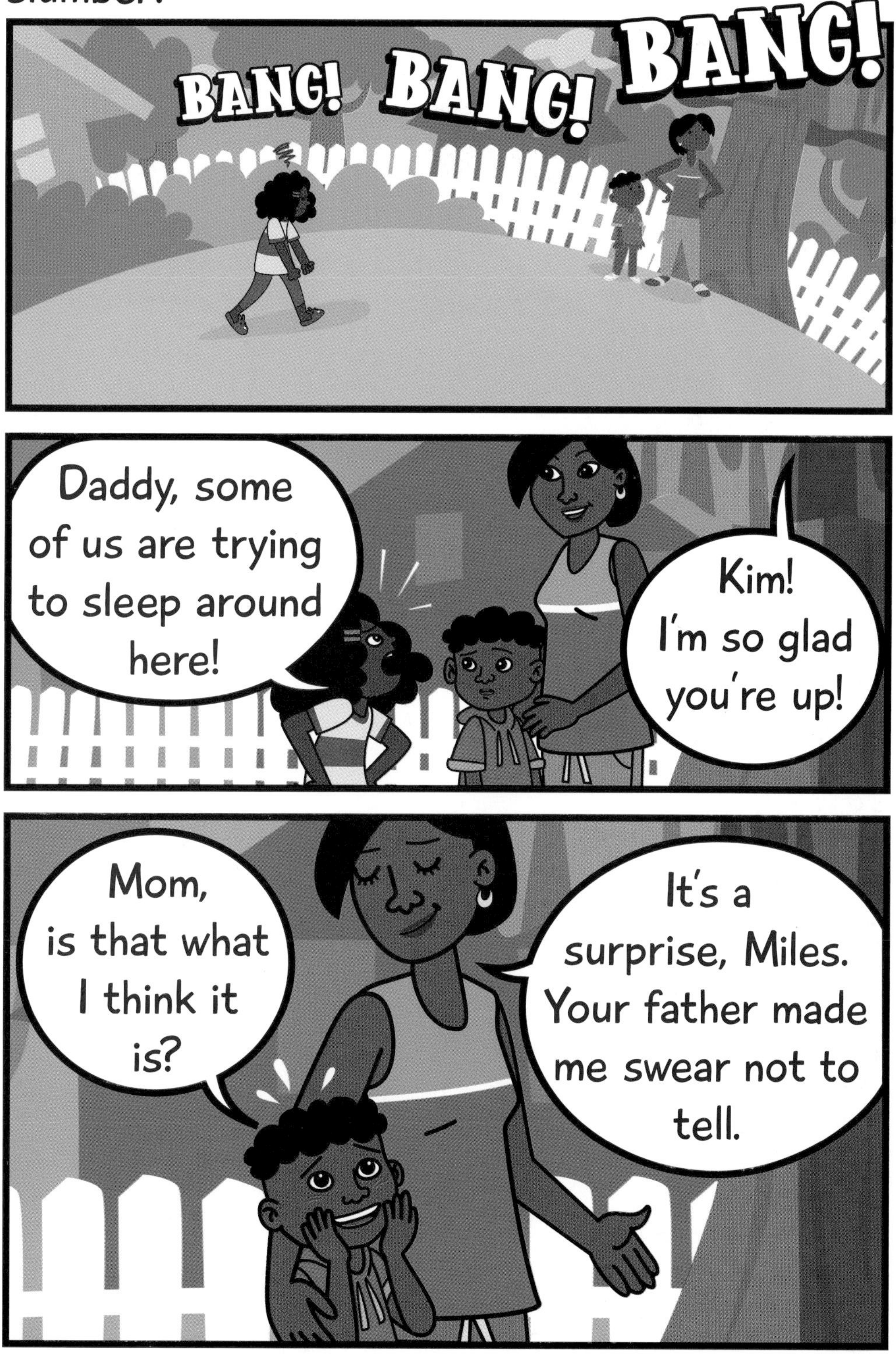
BANG! BANG! BANG!
Daddy, some of us are trying to sleep around here!
Kim! I'm so glad you're up!
Mom, is that what I think it is?
It's a surprise, Miles. Your father made me swear not to tell.

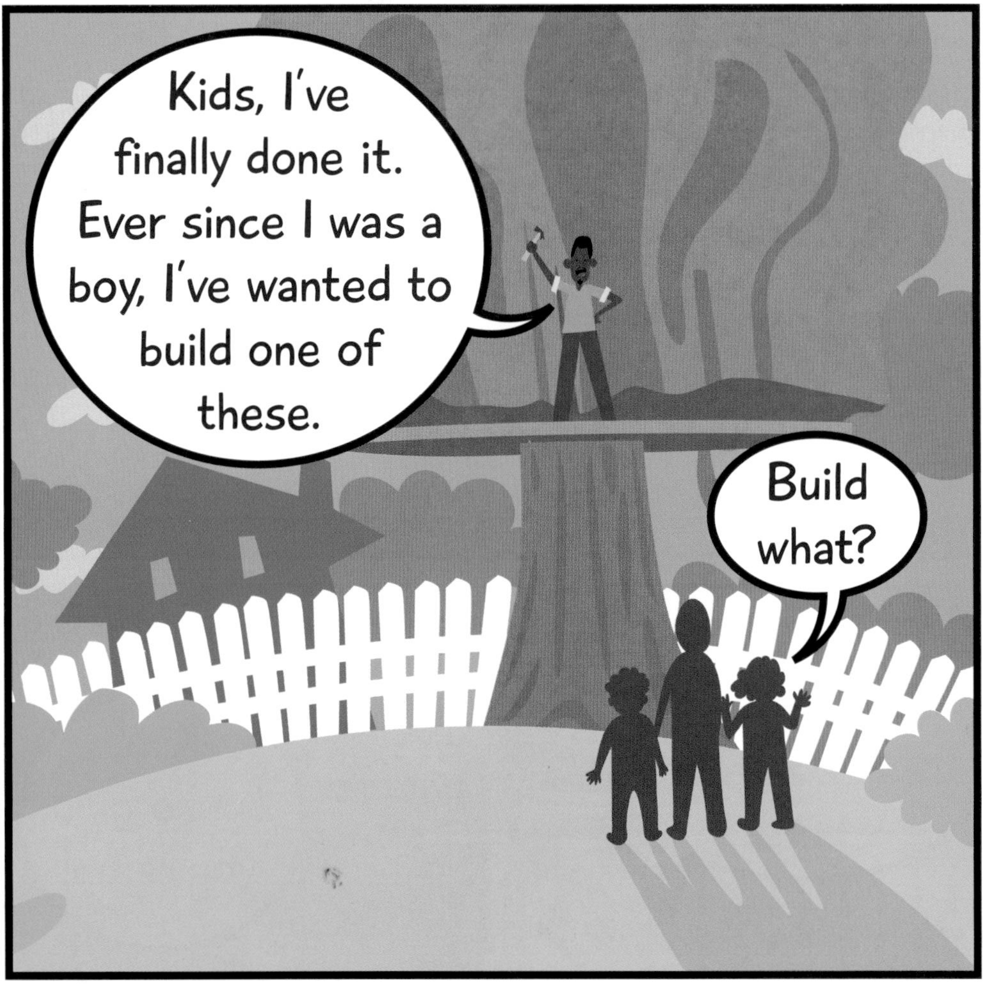
Kids, I've finally done it. Ever since I was a boy, I've wanted to build one of these.
Build what?

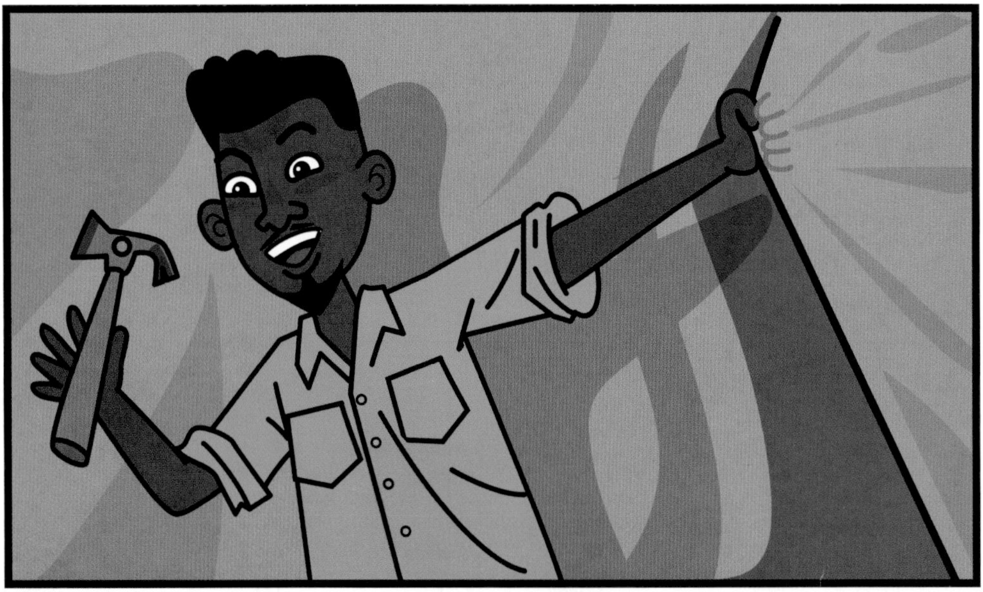

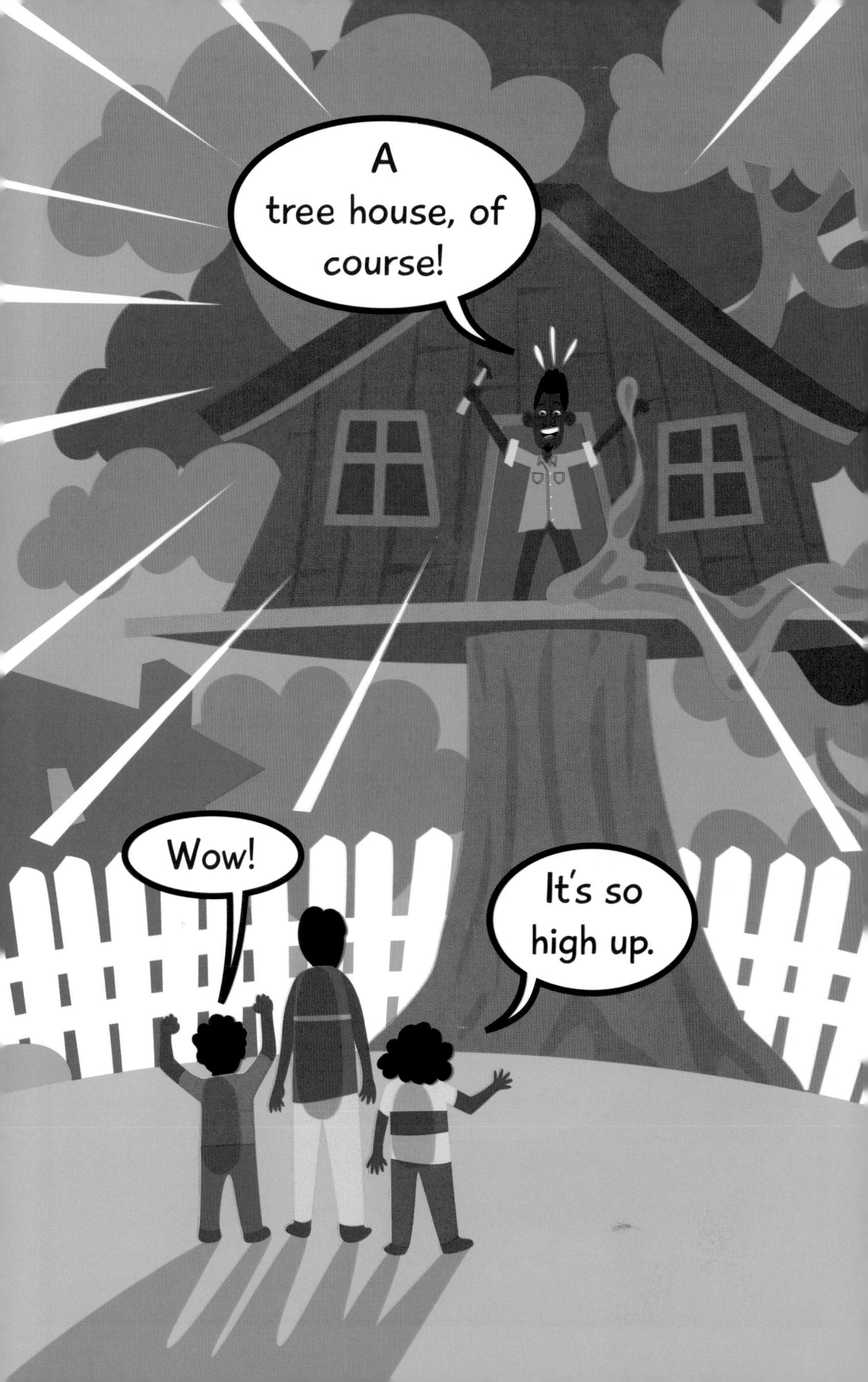
A tree house, of course!
Wow!
It's so high up.

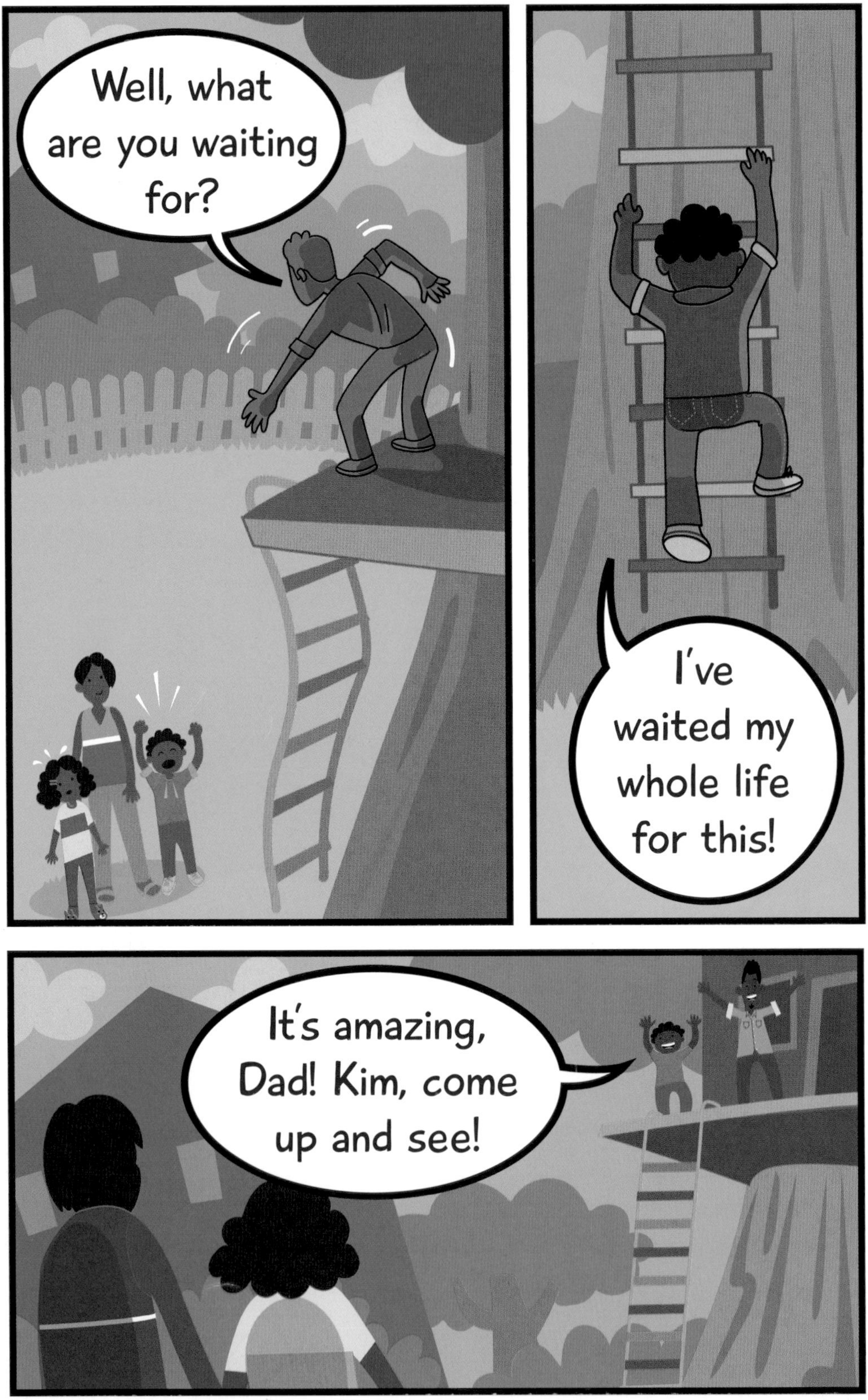
Well, what are you waiting for?
I've waited my whole life for this!
It's amazing, Dad! Kim, come up and see!

Miles made it look so easy. But to Kim, the tree house seems a million feet high.

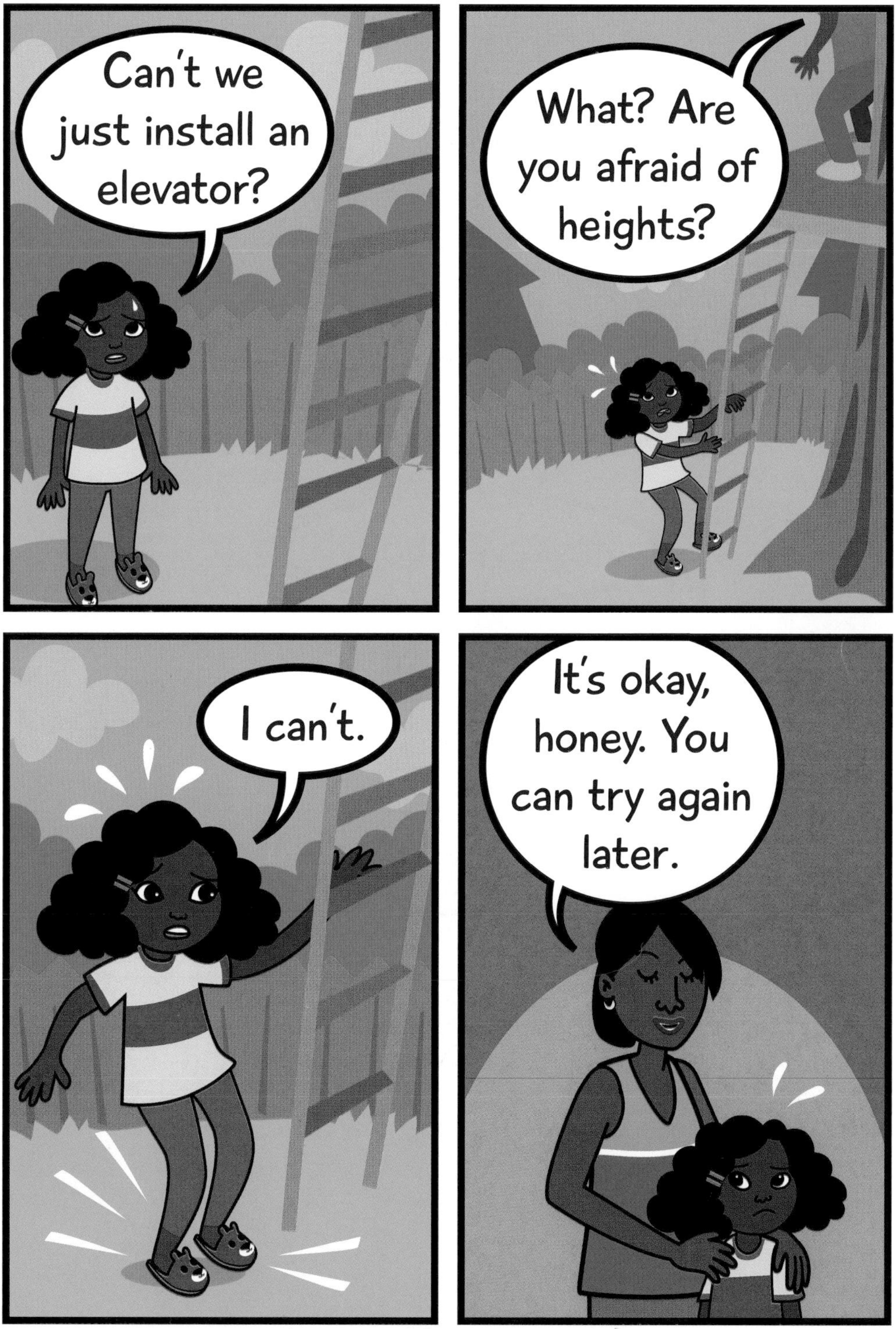
Can't we just install an elevator?
What? Are you afraid of heights?
I can't.
It's okay, honey. You can try again later.

Kim and Miles love riding their bicycles to school.

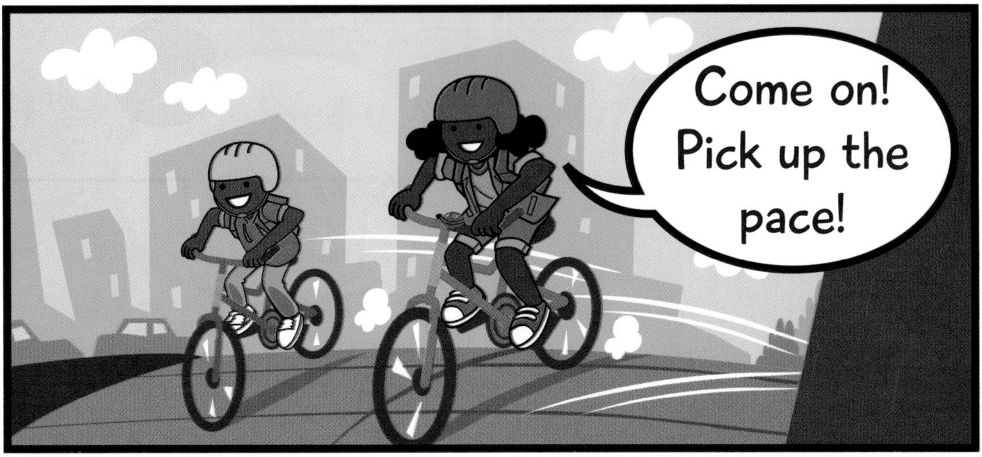
Come on! Pick up the pace!

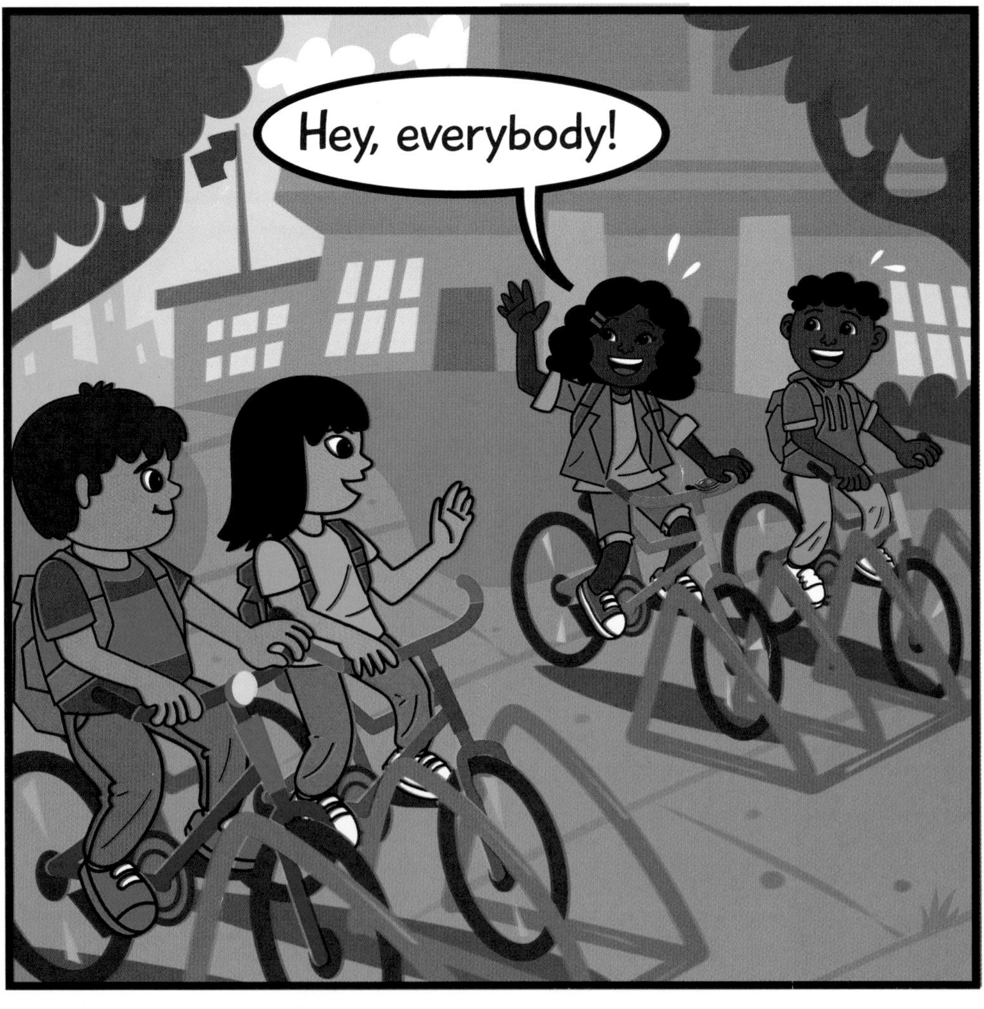
Hey, everybody!

All the kids in Fairville pedal their bicycles to school.

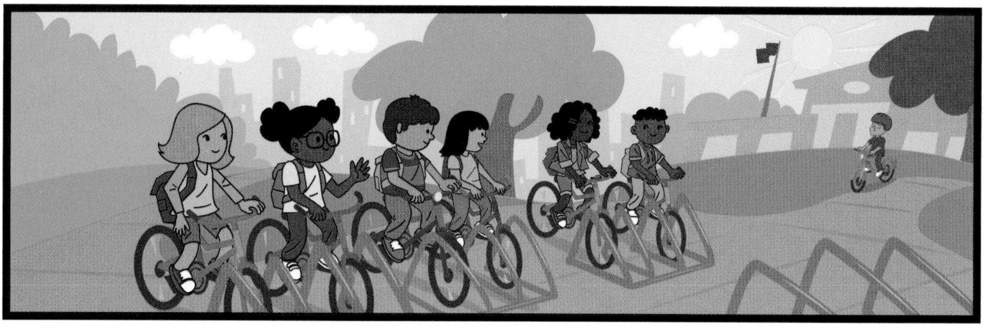

Except for Neil Strong. His electric bicycle does the pedaling for him.

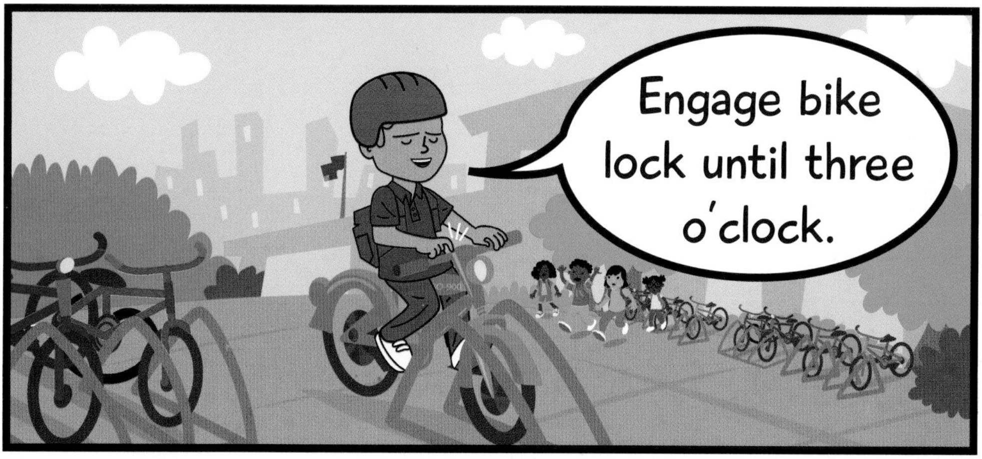
Engage bike lock until three o'clock.

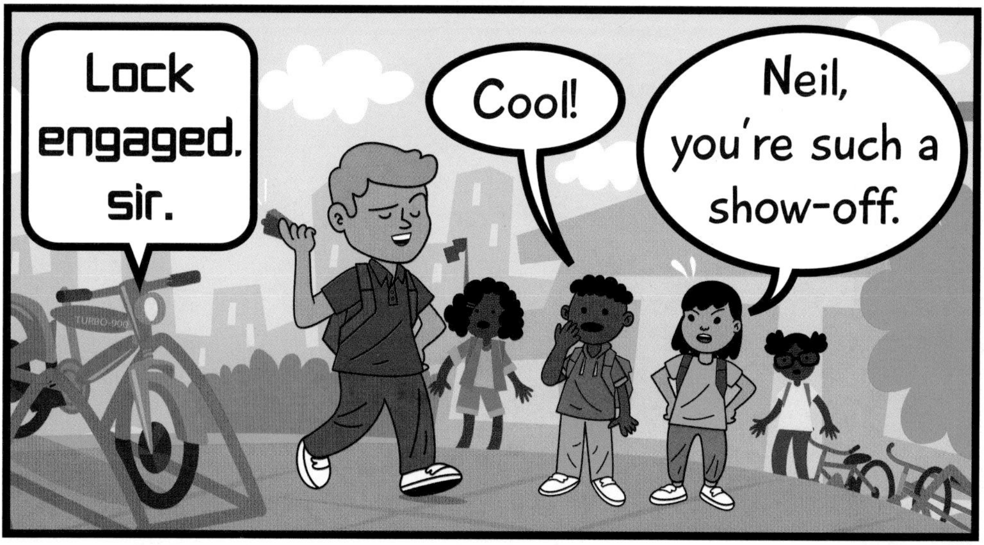
Lock engaged. sir.
Cool!
Neil, you're such a show-off.

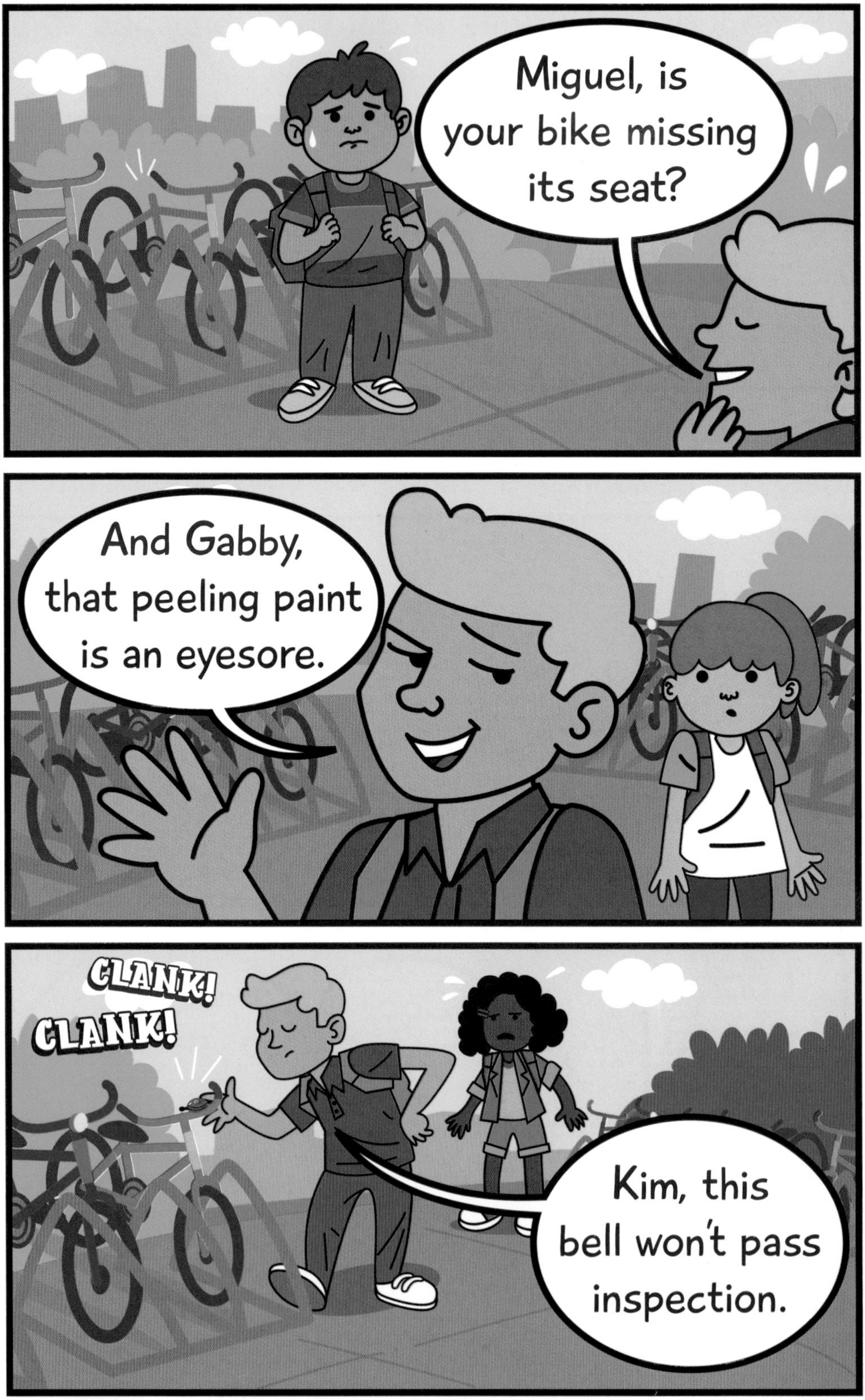
Miguel, is your bike missing its seat?
And Gabby, that peeling paint is an eyesore.
CLANK!
CLANK!
Kim, this bell won't pass inspection.

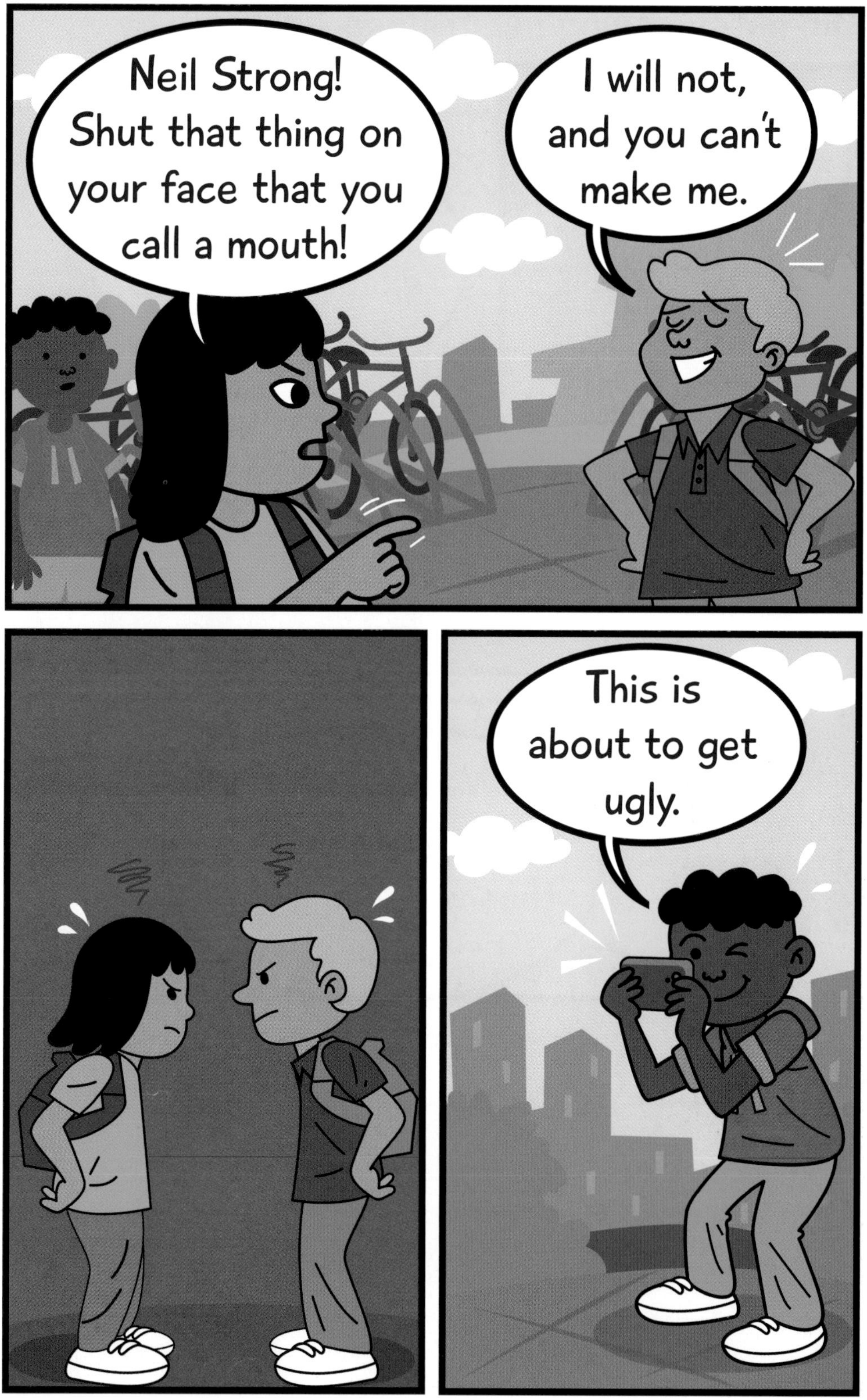
Neil Strong! Shut that thing on your face that you call a mouth!
I will not, and you can't make me.
This is about to get ugly.

Kim hates seeing her friends fight.

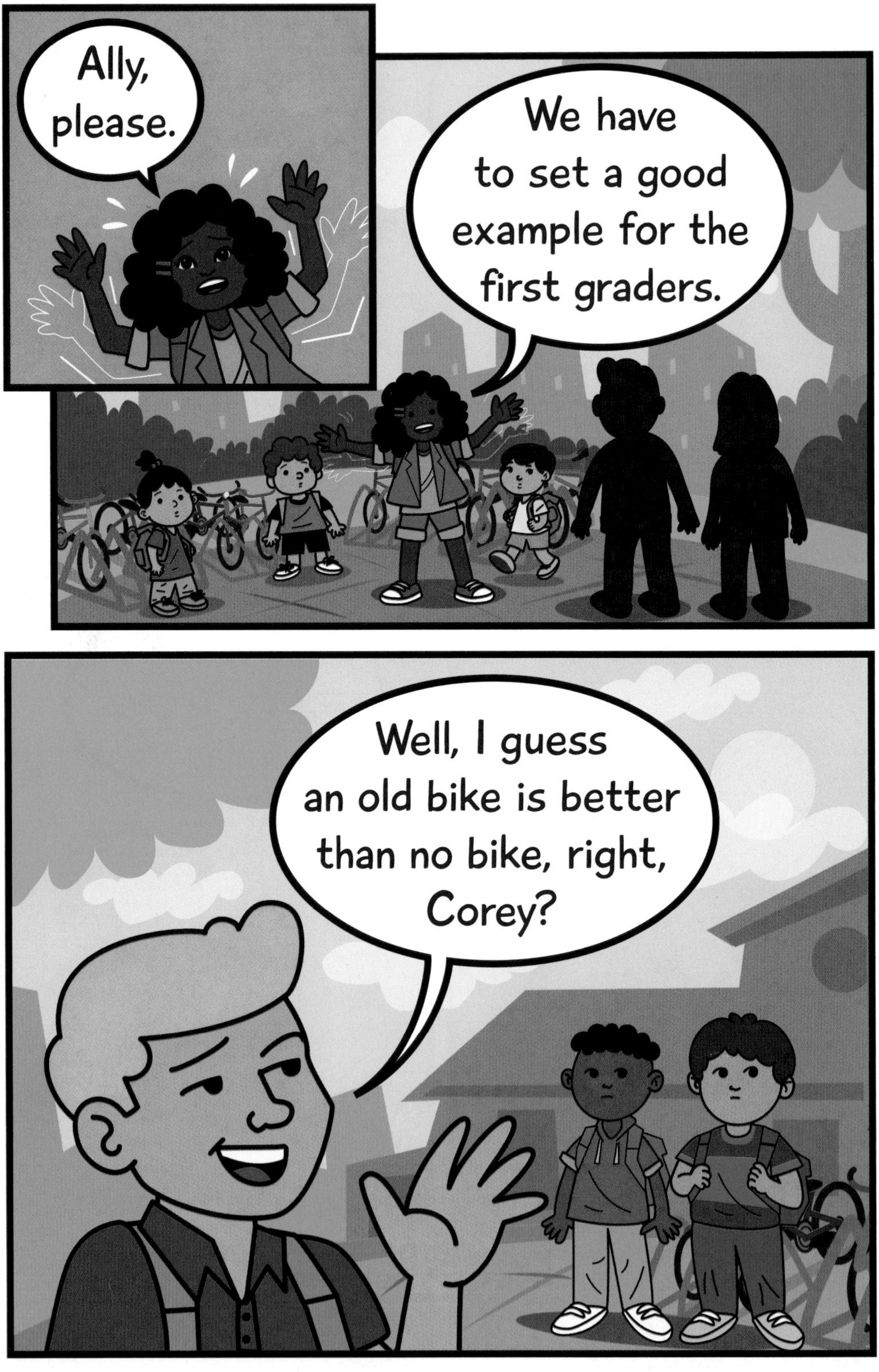
Ally, please.
We have to set a good example for the first graders.
Well, I guess an old bike is better than no bike, right, Corey?

Corey Boone is the new kid at school.

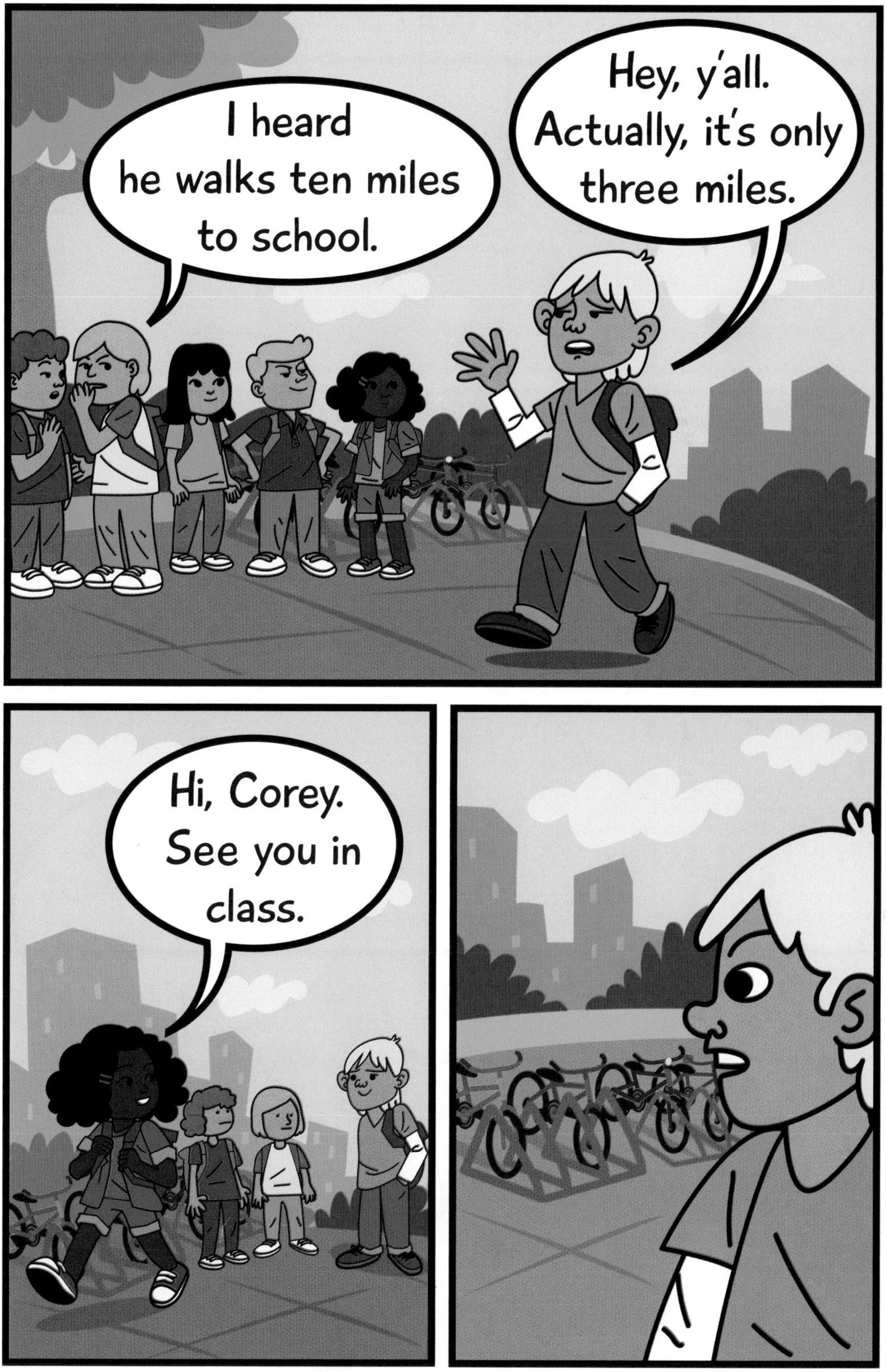
I heard he walks ten miles to school.
Hey, y'all. Actually, it's only three miles.
Hi, Corey. See you in class.

After school, the kids happily run outside to get their bicycles. But...

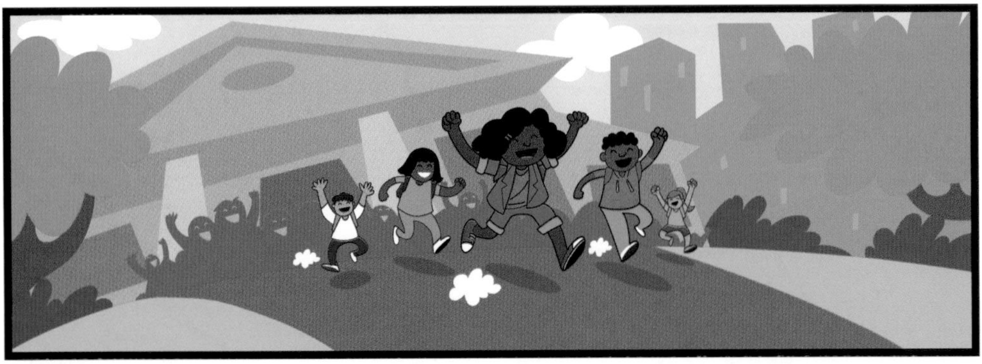

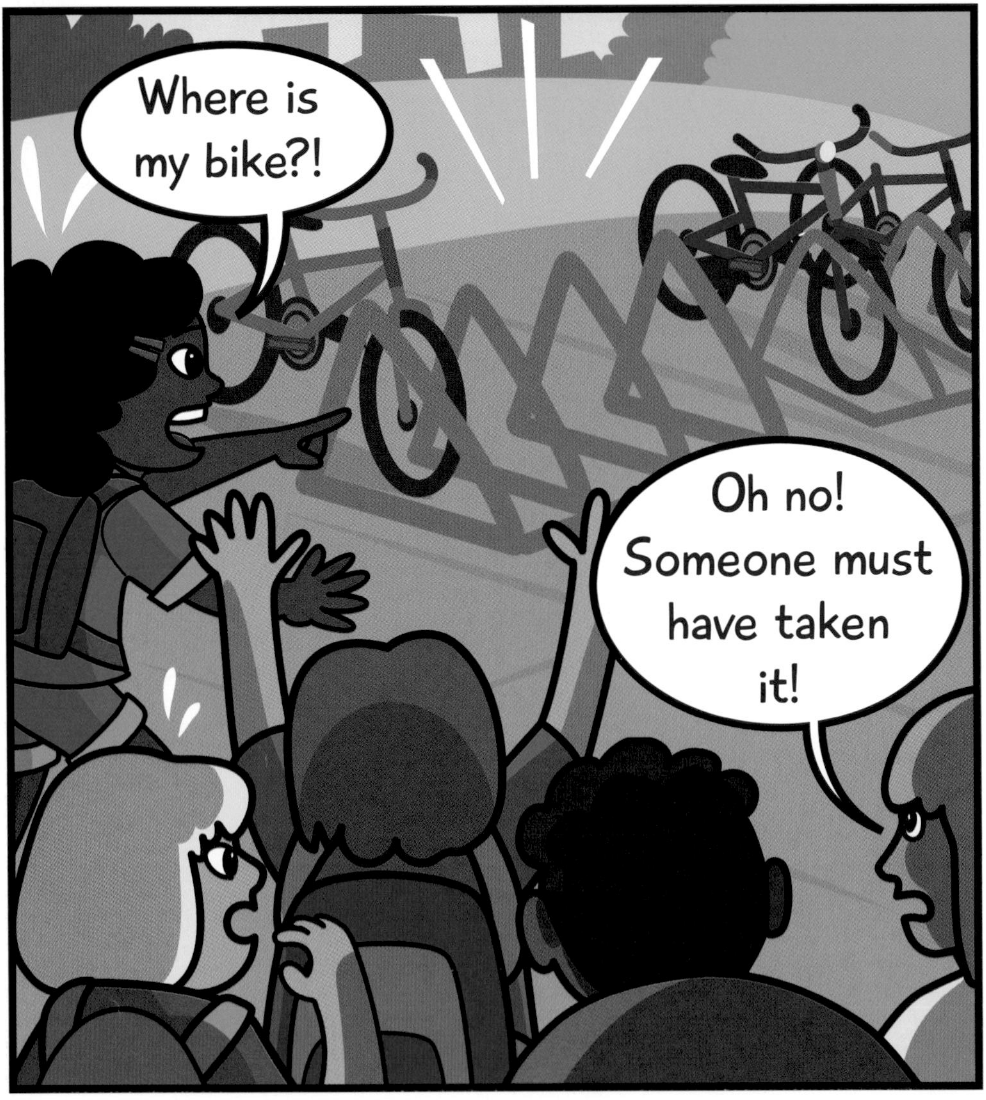
Where is my bike?!
Oh no! Someone must have taken it!

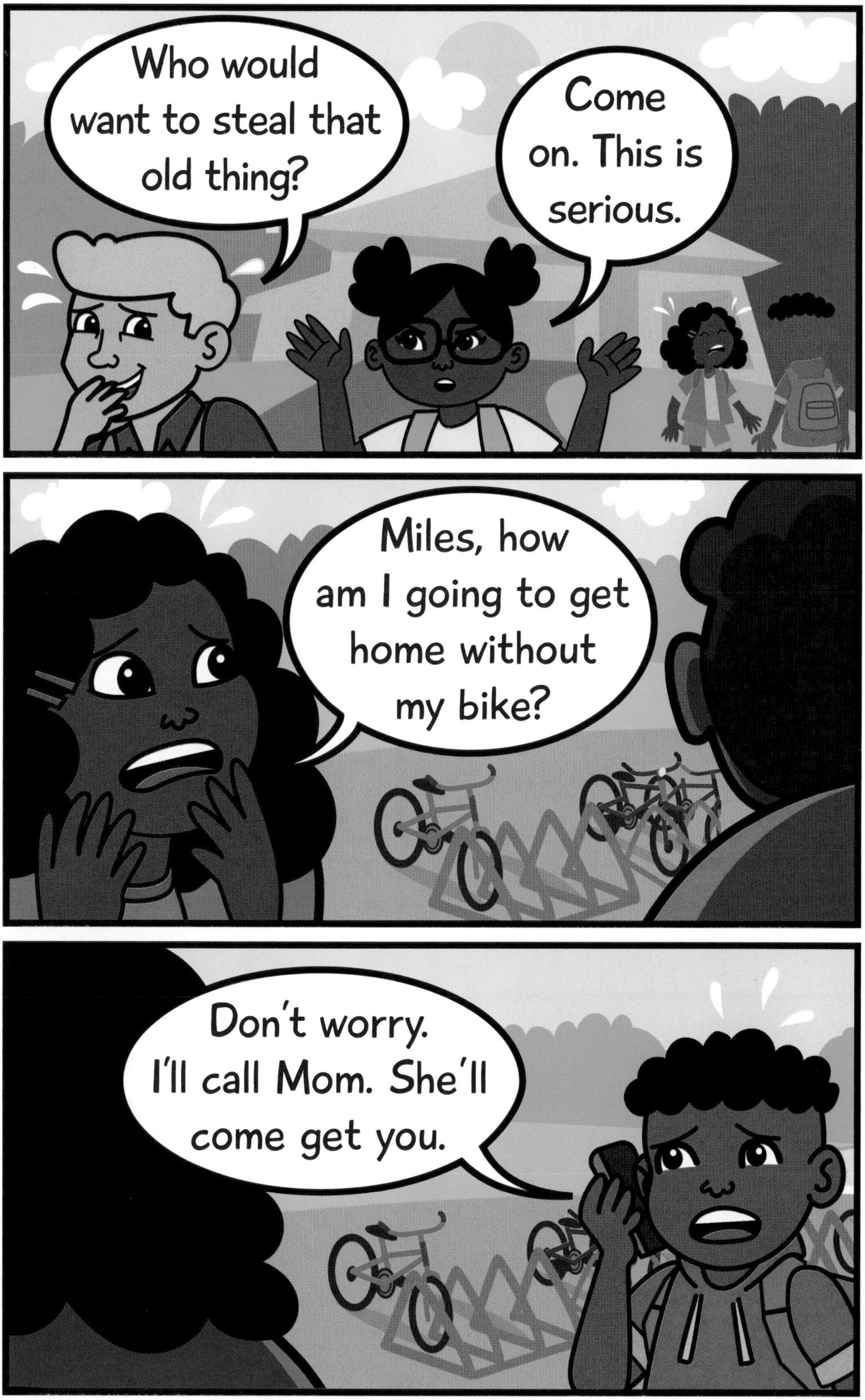
Who would want to steal that old thing?
Come on. This is serious.
Miles, how am I going to get home without my bike?
Don't worry. I'll call Mom. She'll come get you.

A short while later...

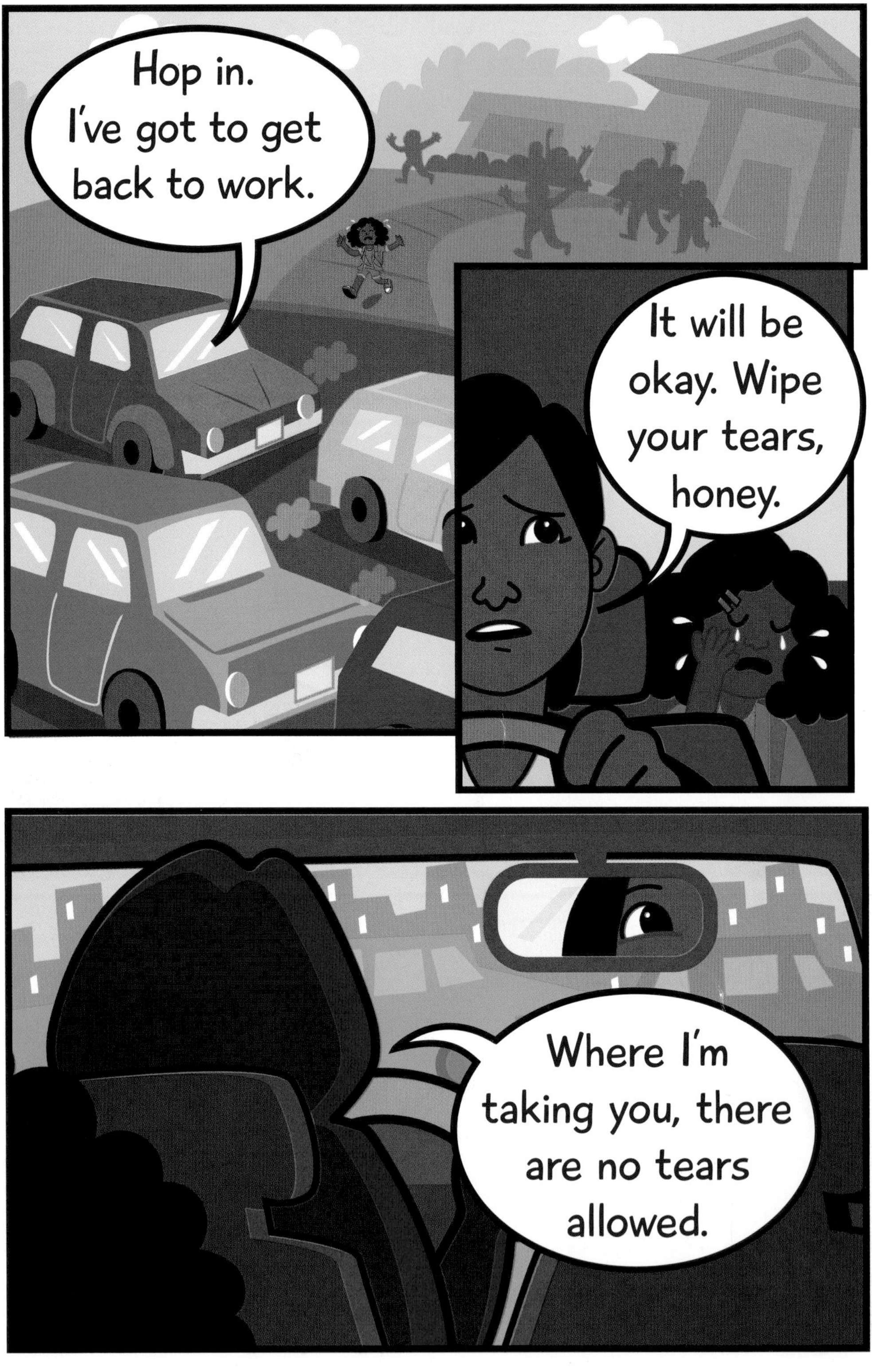
Hop in. I've got to get back to work.
It will be okay. Wipe your tears, honey.
Where I'm taking you, there are no tears allowed.

Welcome to the Fairville Courthouse! This is where Kim's mother works as a judge.

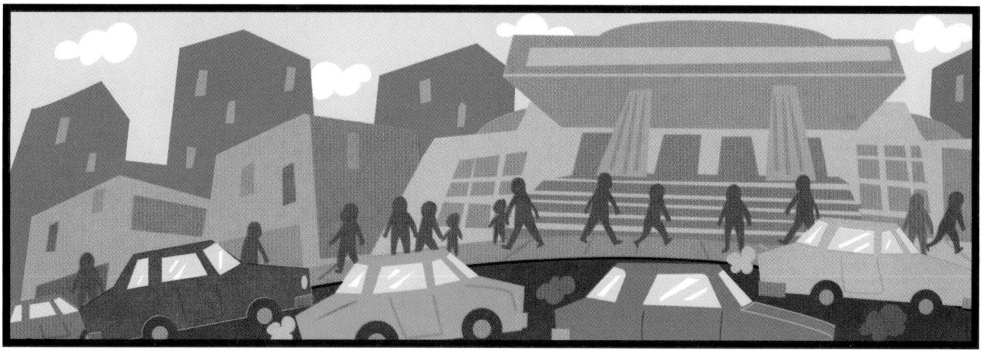

When people have a disagreement, they come to the judge for help.

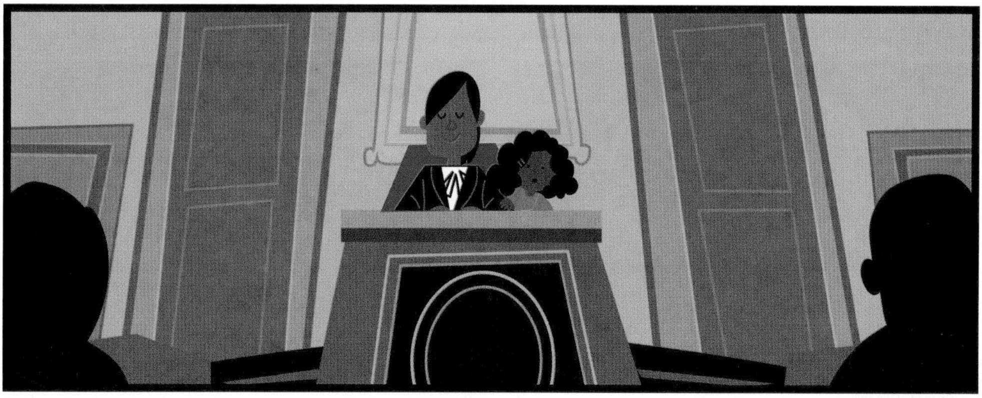

She listens to both sides of the story. Then she looks at all the facts and evidence before deciding who is right and who is wrong.

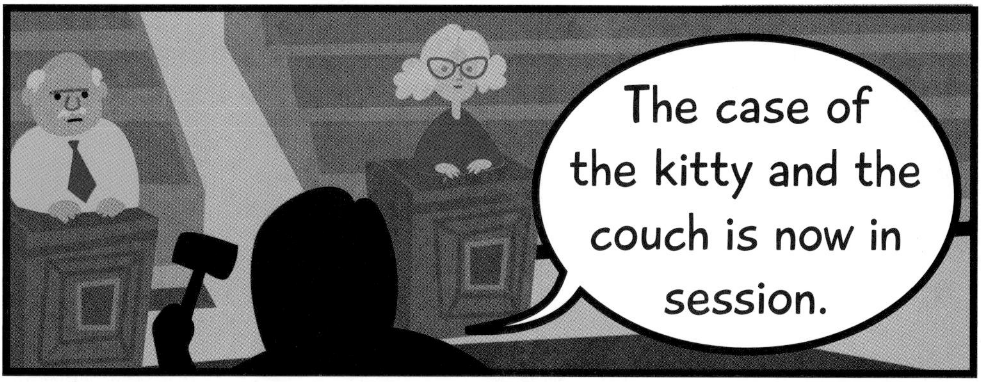
The case of the kitty and the couch is now in session.

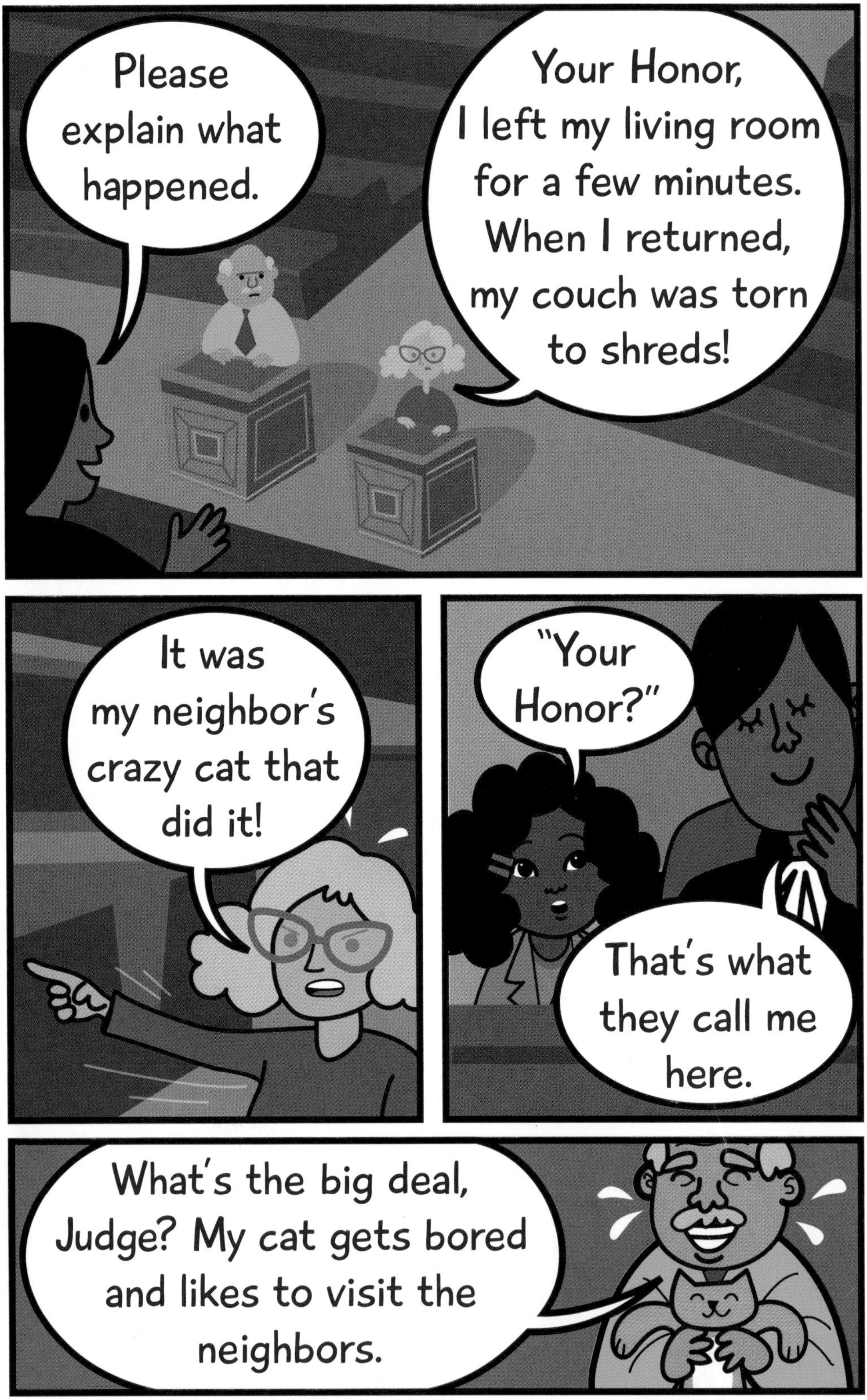
Please explain what happened.
Your Honor, I left my living room for a few minutes. When I returned, my couch was torn to shreds!
It was my neighbor's crazy cat that did it!
"Your Honor?"
That's what they call me here.
What's the big deal, Judge? My cat gets bored and likes to visit the neighbors.

Before her mom decides on the case, she wants to hear what Kim thinks.

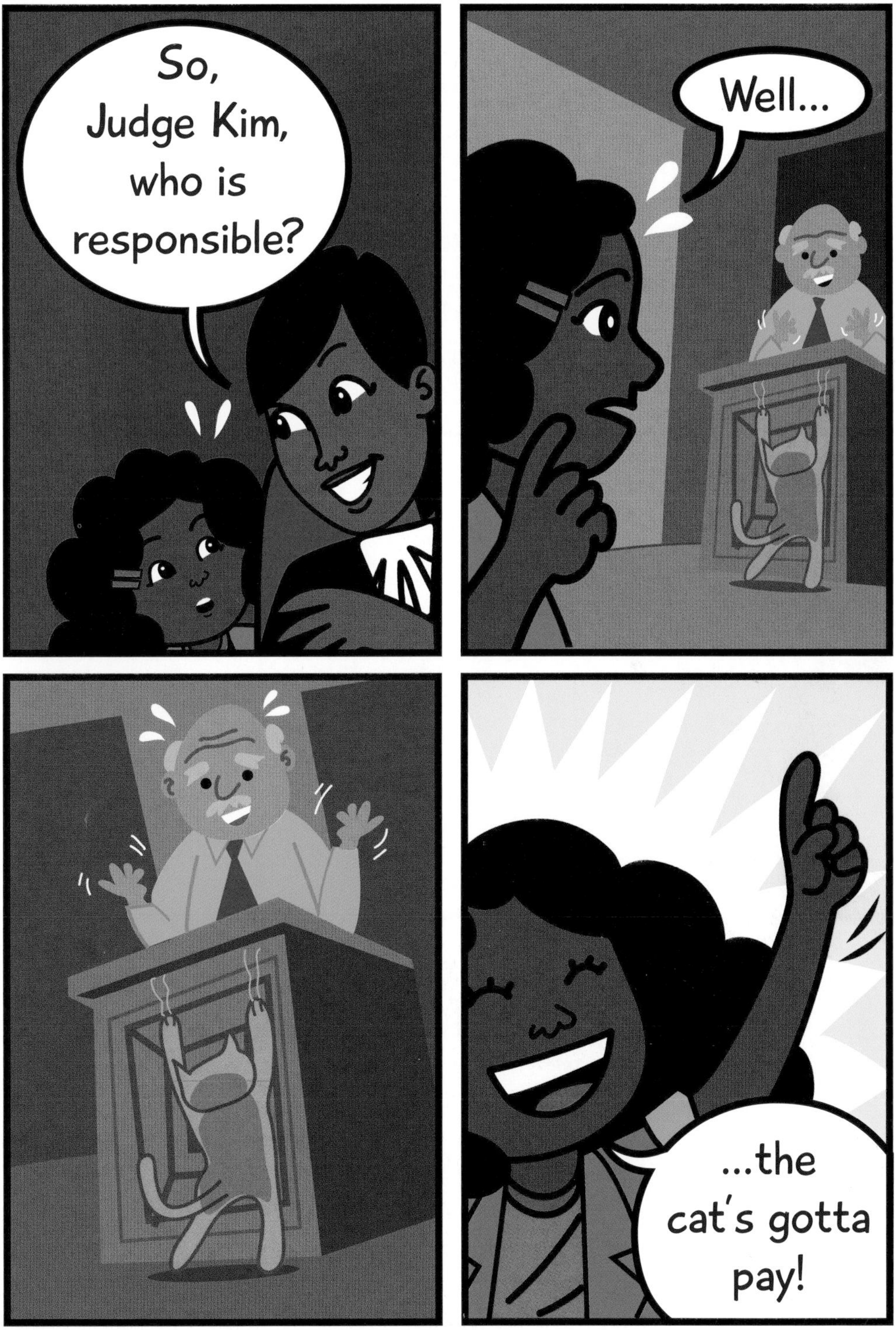
So, Judge Kim, who is responsible?
Well...
...the cat's gotta pay!

At dinner Kim tells Miles about her day.

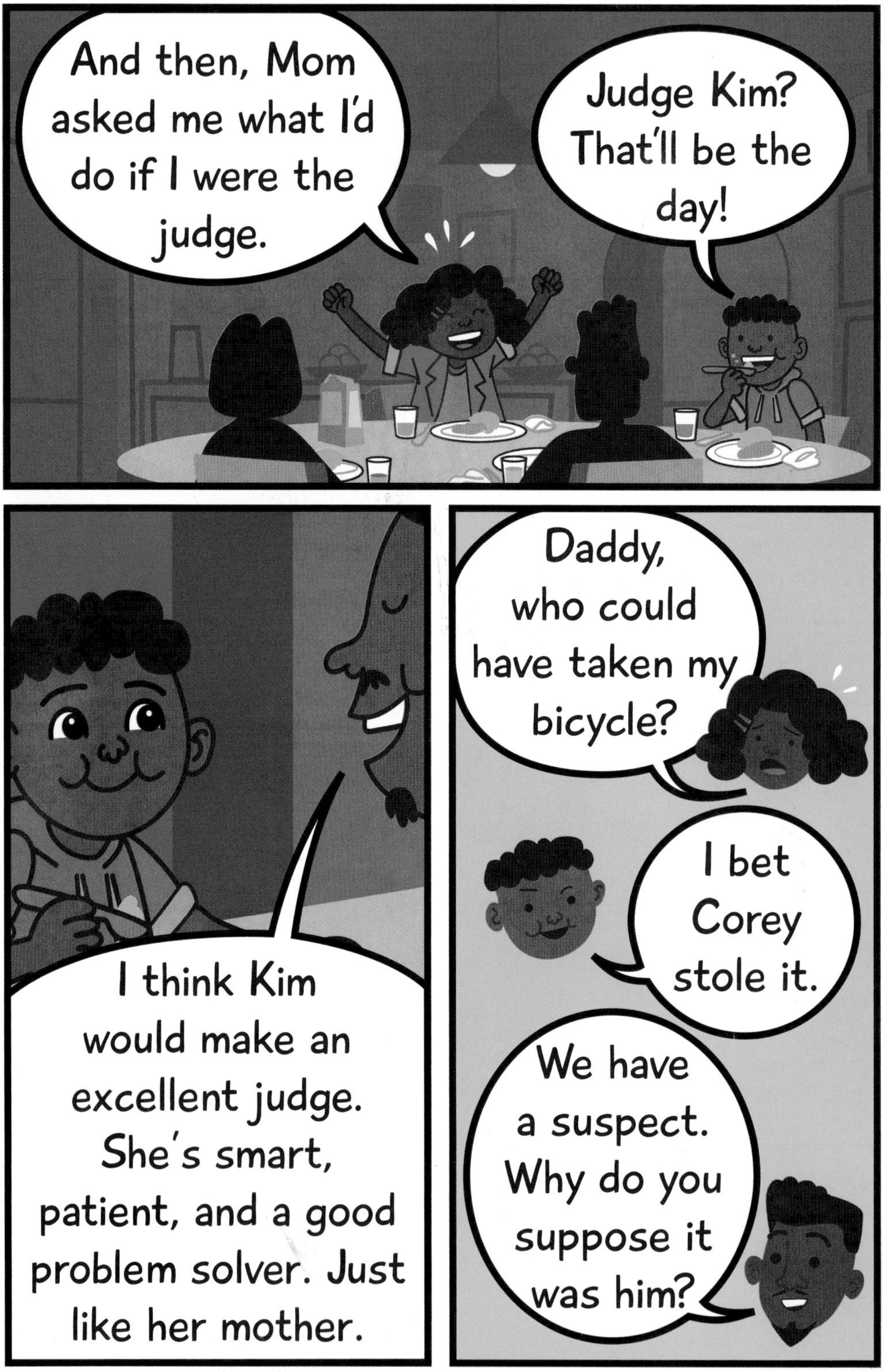
And then, Mom asked me what I'd do if I were the judge.
Judge Kim? That'll be the day!
I think Kim would make an excellent judge. She's smart, patient, and a good problem solver. Just like her mother.
Daddy, who could have taken my bicycle?
I bet Corey stole it.
We have a suspect. Why do you suppose it was him?

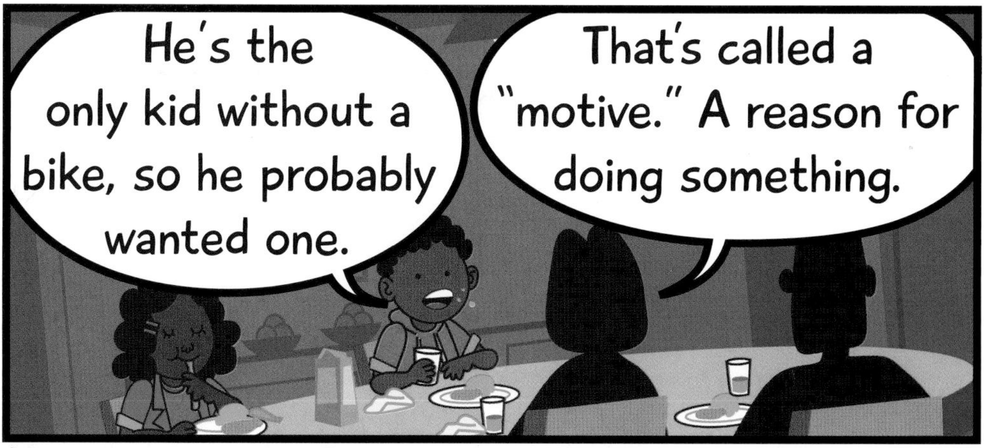
He's the only kid without a bike, so he probably wanted one.
That's called a "motive." A reason for doing something.

Kim considers Corey as a suspect, but it doesn't add up.

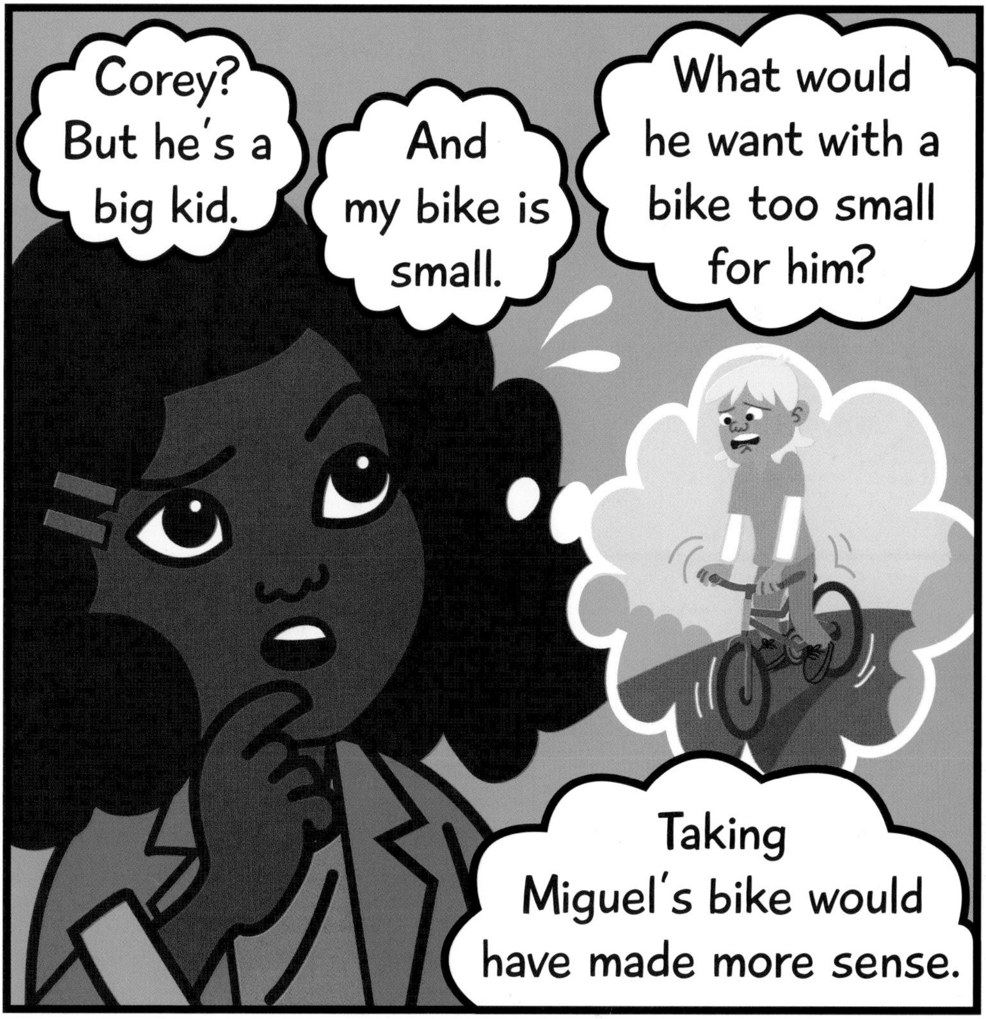
Corey? But he's a big kid.
And my bike is small.
What would he want with a bike too small for him?
Taking Miguel's bike would have made more sense.

The next day at school...

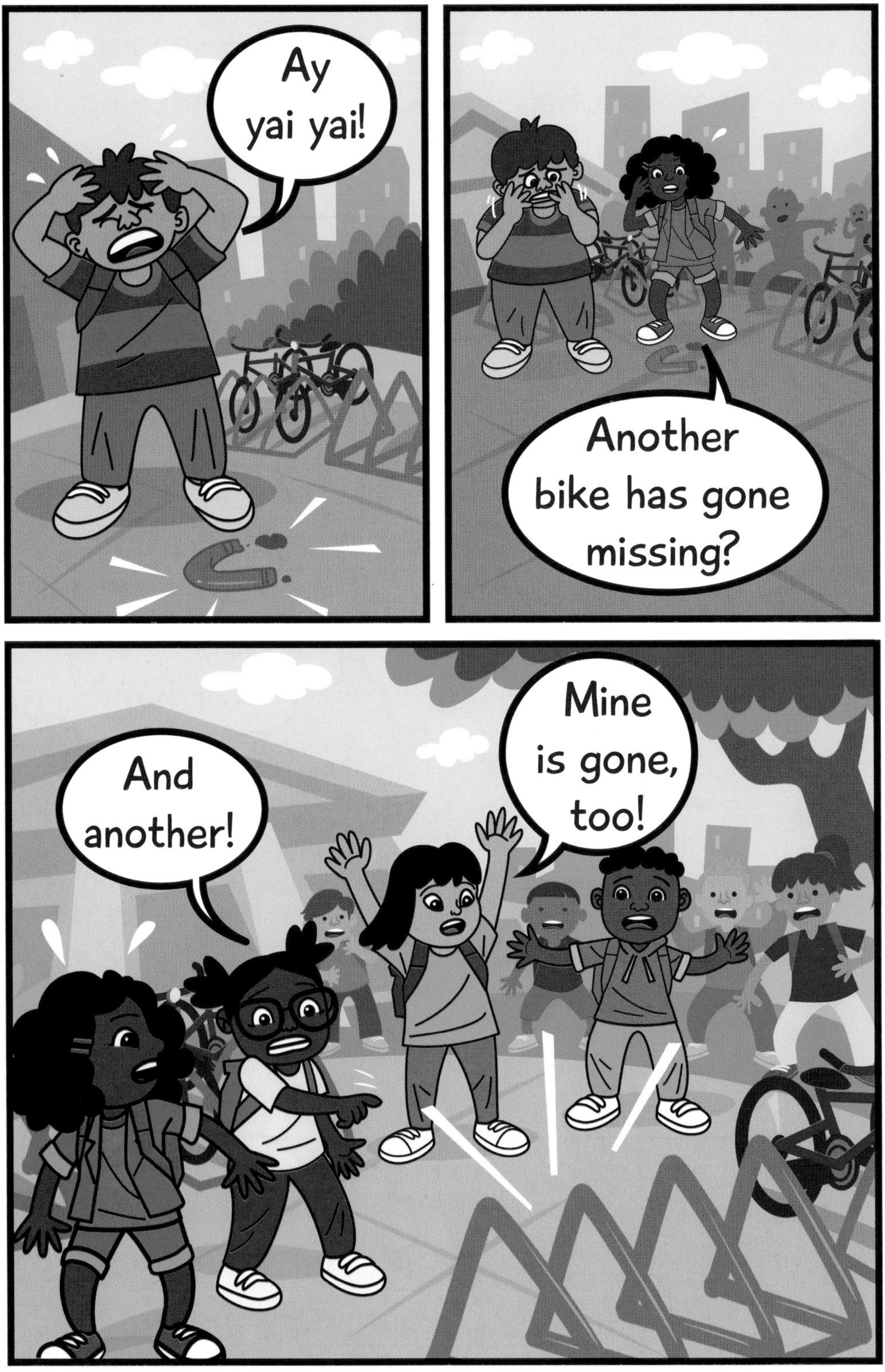
Ay yai yai!
Another bike has gone missing?
And another!
Mine is gone, too!

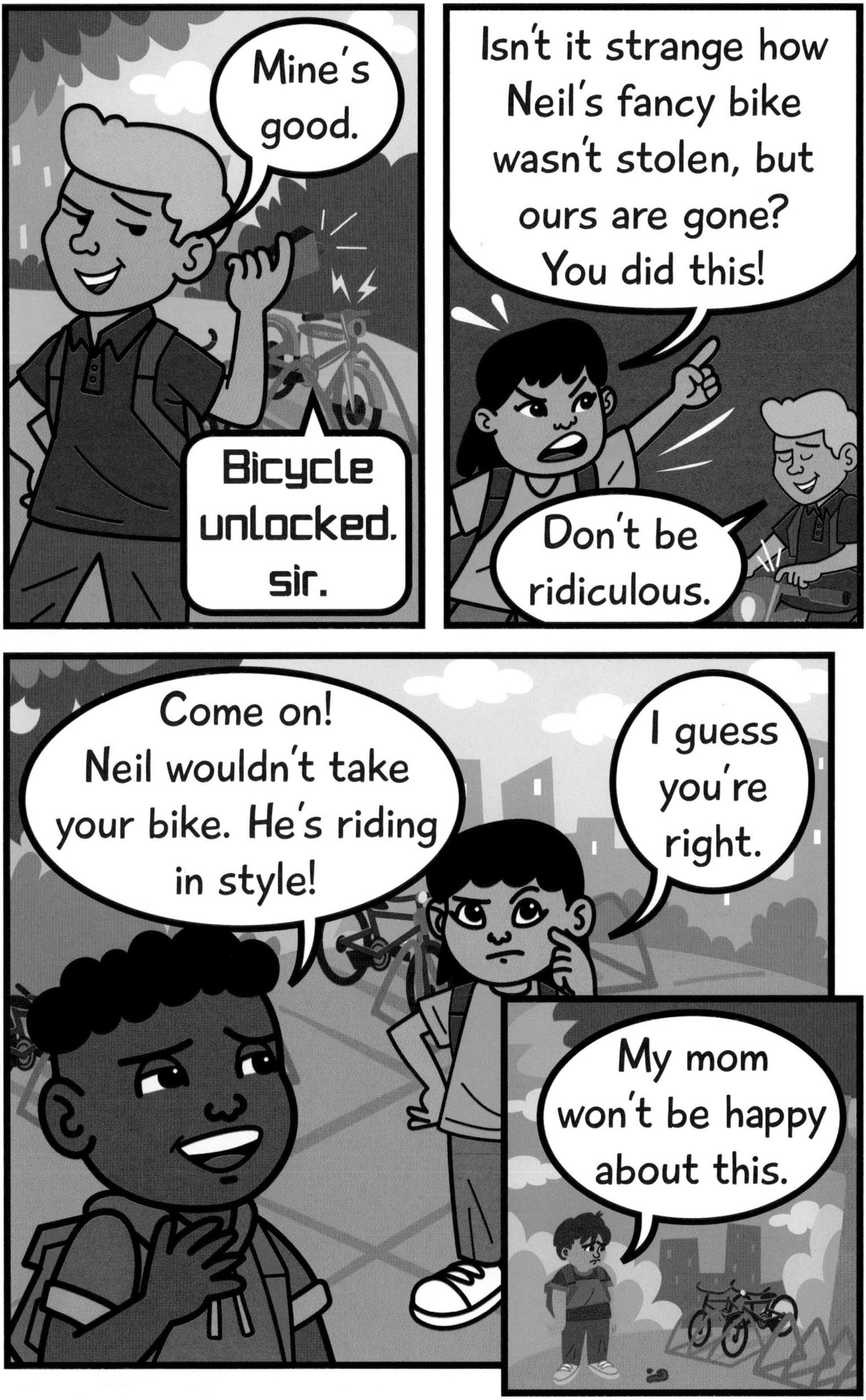
Mine's good.
Bicycle unlocked. sir.
Isn't it strange how Neil's fancy bike wasn't stolen, but ours are gone? You did this!
Don't be ridiculous.
Come on! Neil wouldn't take your bike. He's riding in style!
I guess you're right.
My mom won't be happy about this.

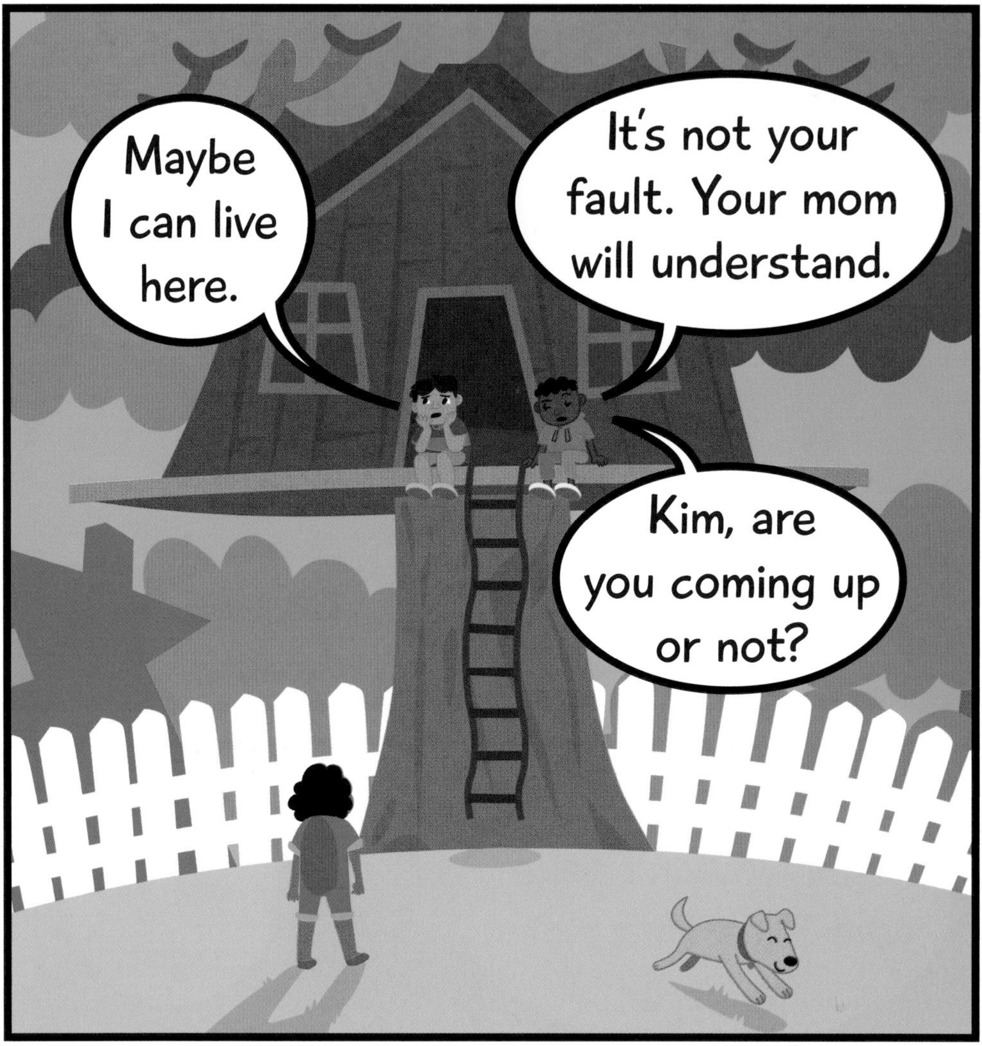
Maybe I can live here.
It's not your fault. Your mom will understand.
Kim, are you coming up or not?

Kim watches the ladder shake and sway.

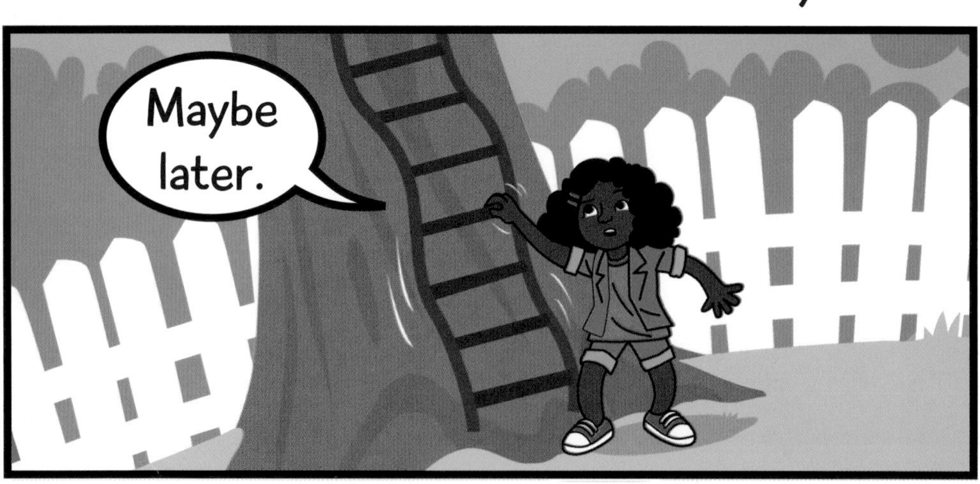
Maybe later.

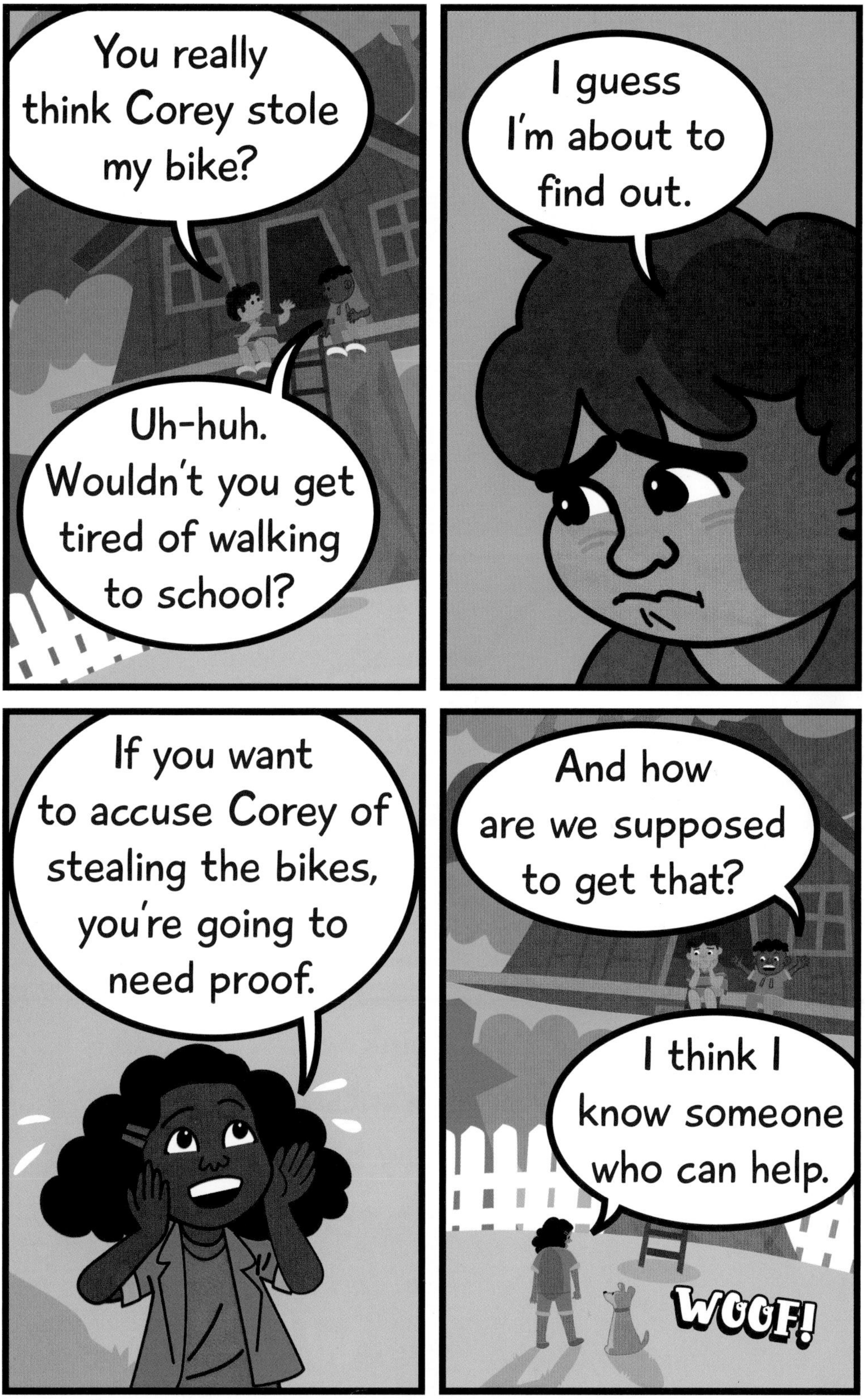
You really think Corey stole my bike?
Uh-huh. Wouldn't you get tired of walking to school?
I guess I'm about to find out.
If you want to accuse Corey of stealing the bikes, you're going to need proof.
And how are we supposed to get that?
I think I know someone who can help.
WOOF!

Taking Kim's advice, the boys bring Digger to school to sniff for clues.

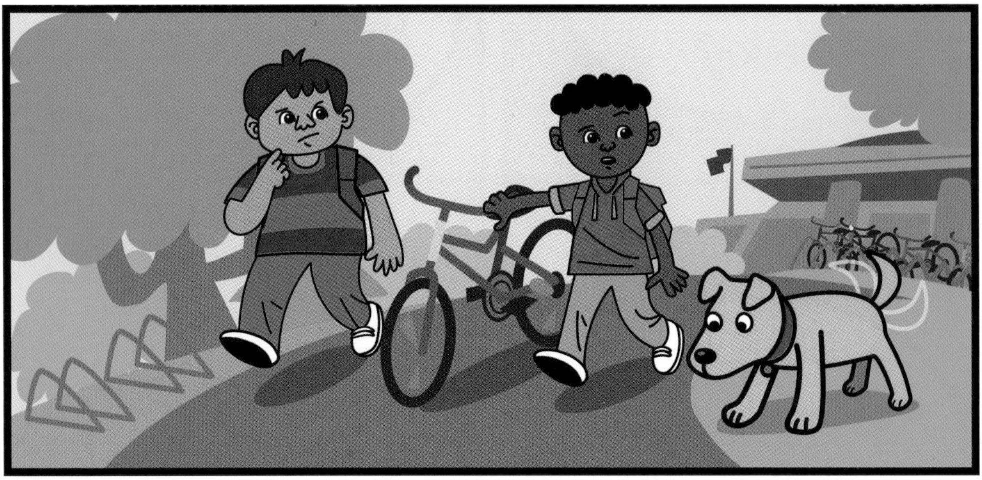

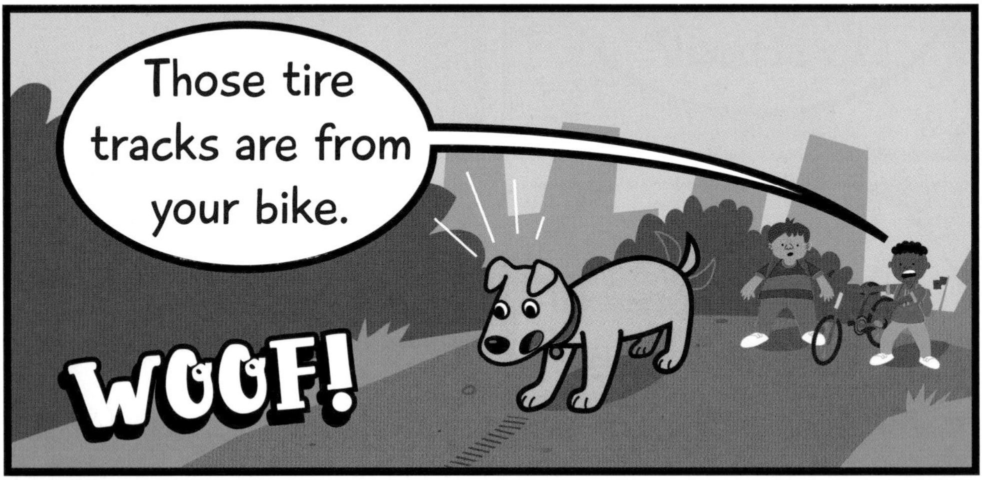
Those tire tracks are from your bike.
WOOF!

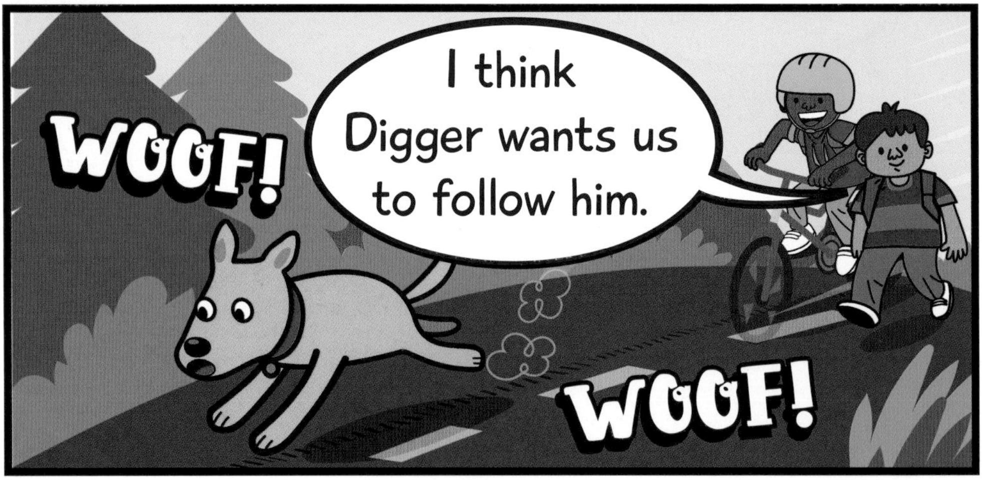
WOOF!
I think Digger wants us to follow him.
WOOF!

The boys follow the tracks through the country hills of Fairville until...

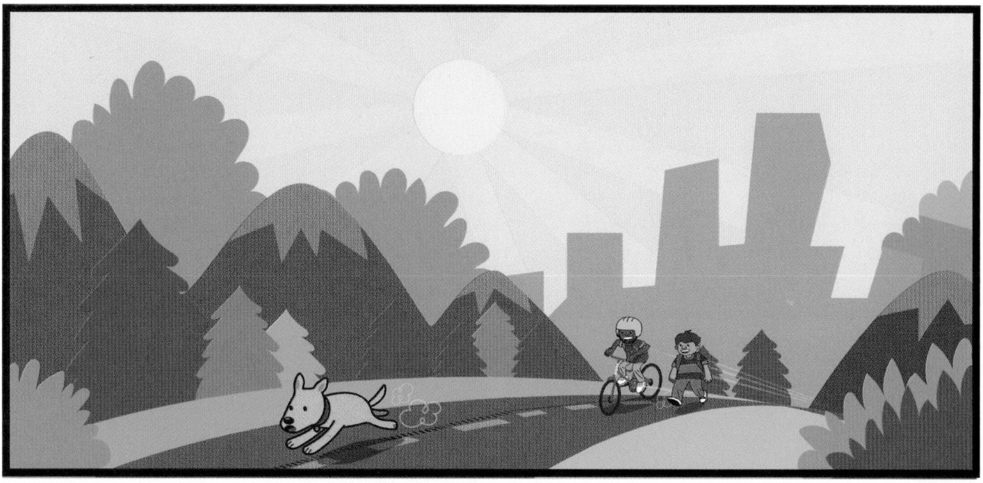

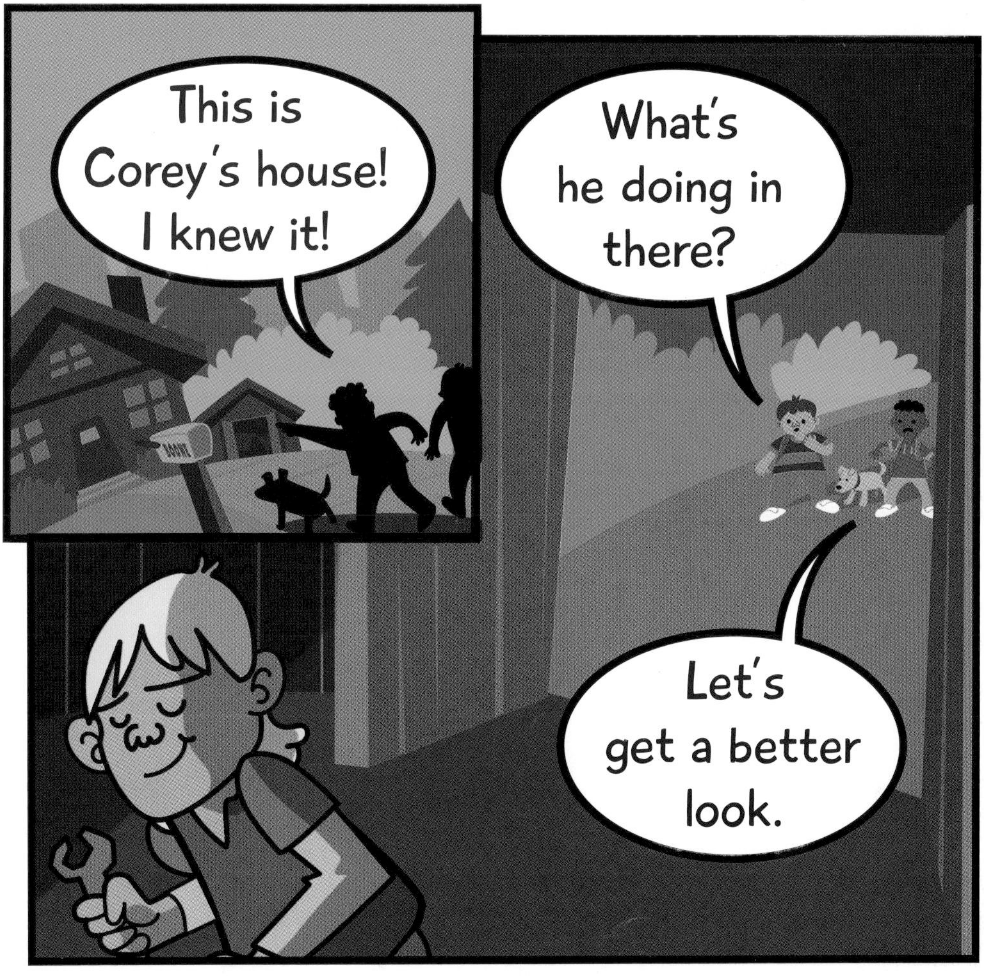
This is Corey's house! I knew it!
What's he doing in there?
Let's get a better look.

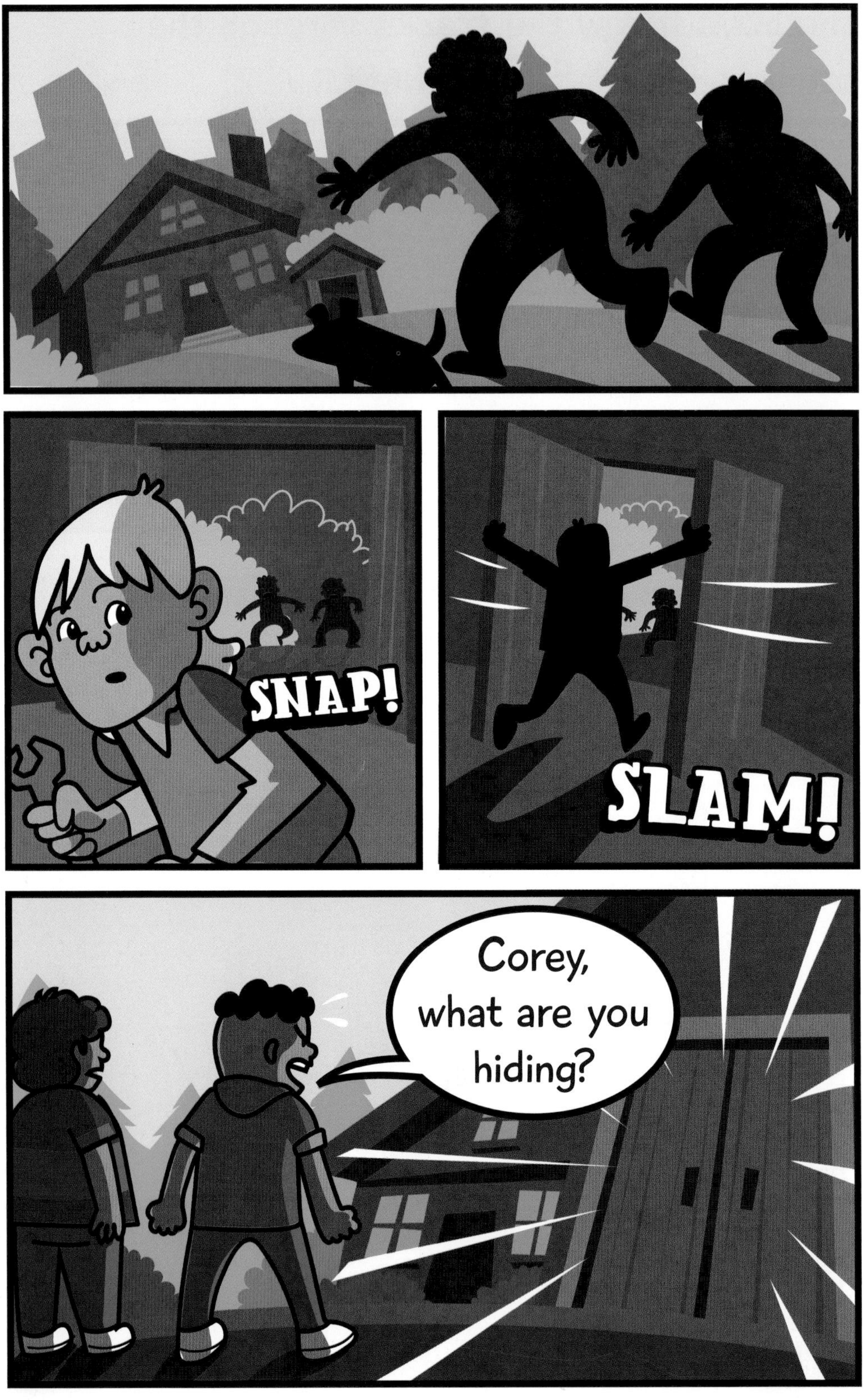
SNAP!
SLAM!
Corey, what are you hiding?

The next day at school...

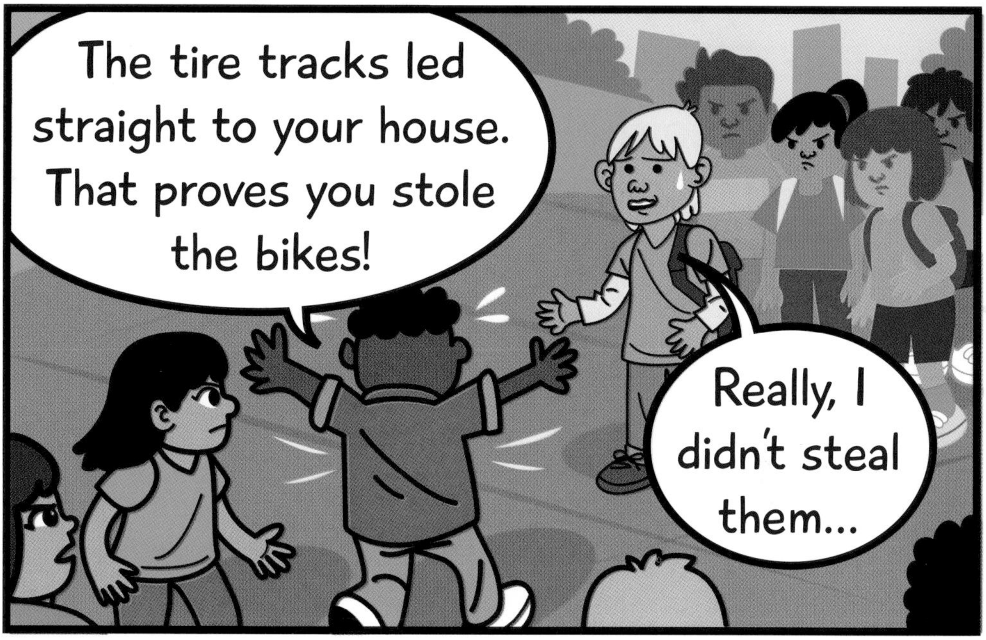
The tire tracks led straight to your house. That proves you stole the bikes!
Really, I didn't steal them...

Corey tries to explain, but the other kids won't listen.

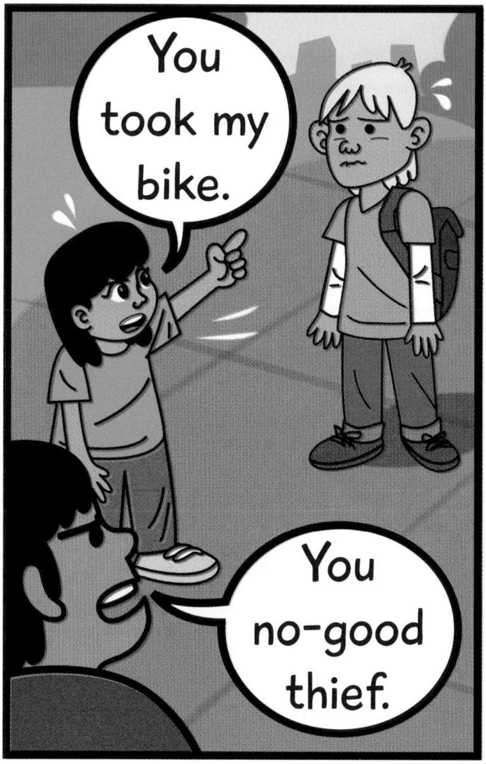
You took my bike.
You no-good thief.

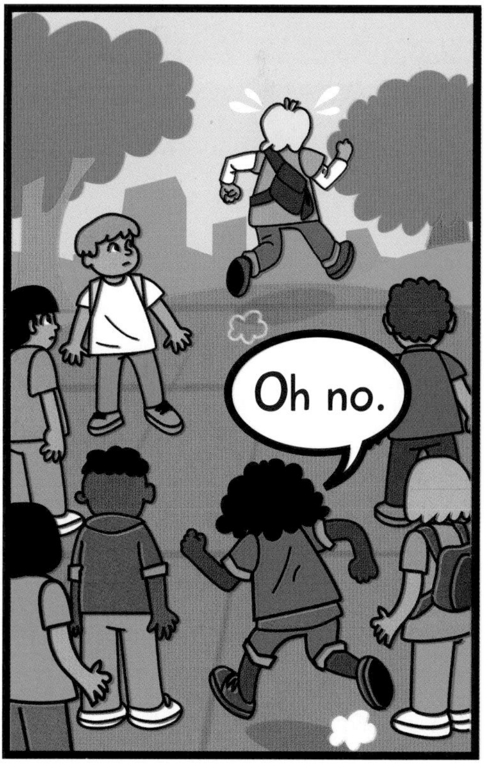
Oh no.

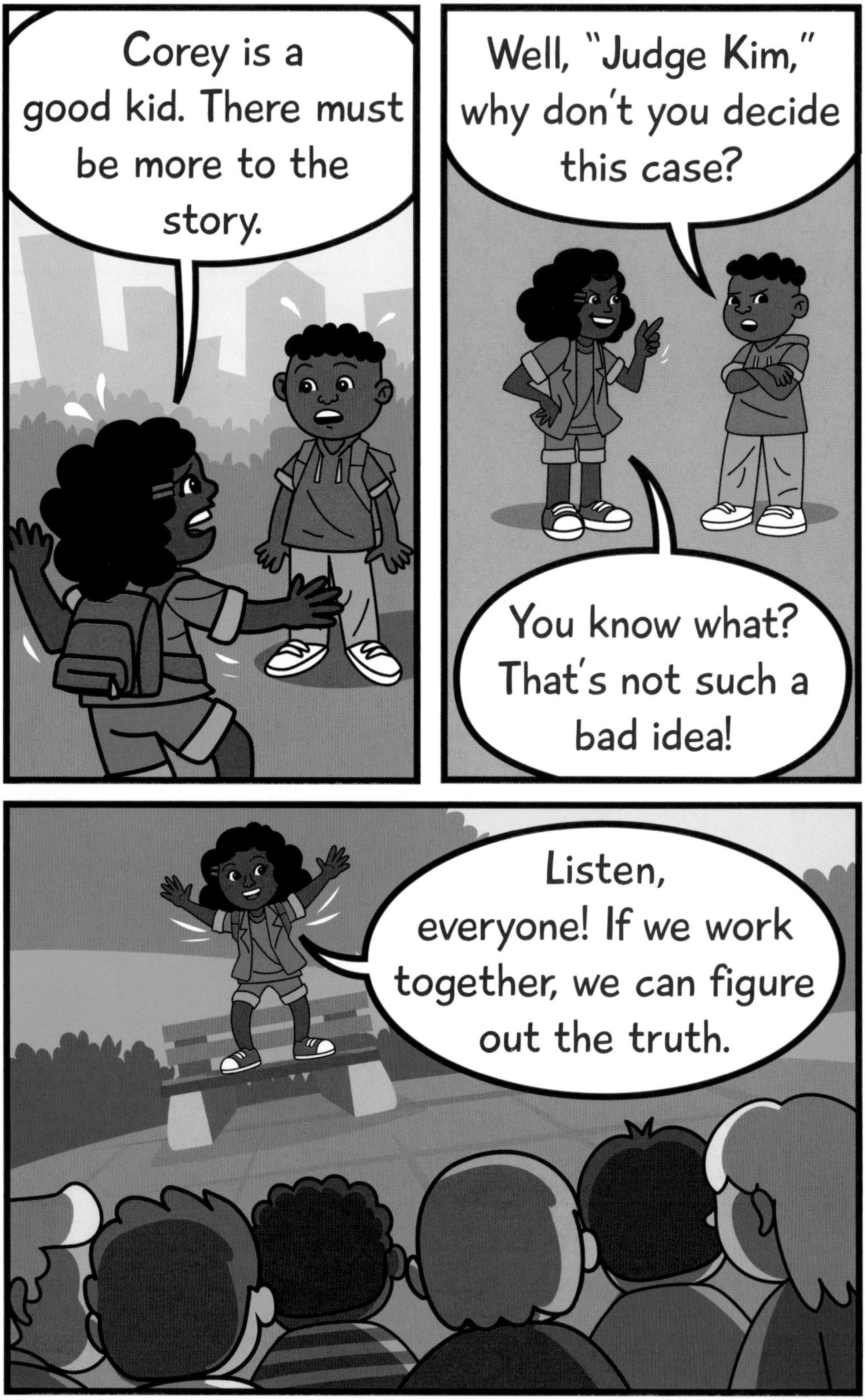
Corey is a good kid. There must be more to the story.
Well, "Judge Kim," why don't you decide this case?
You know what? That's not such a bad idea!
Listen, everyone! If we work together, we can figure out the truth.

Kim gives each of her friends an important job.

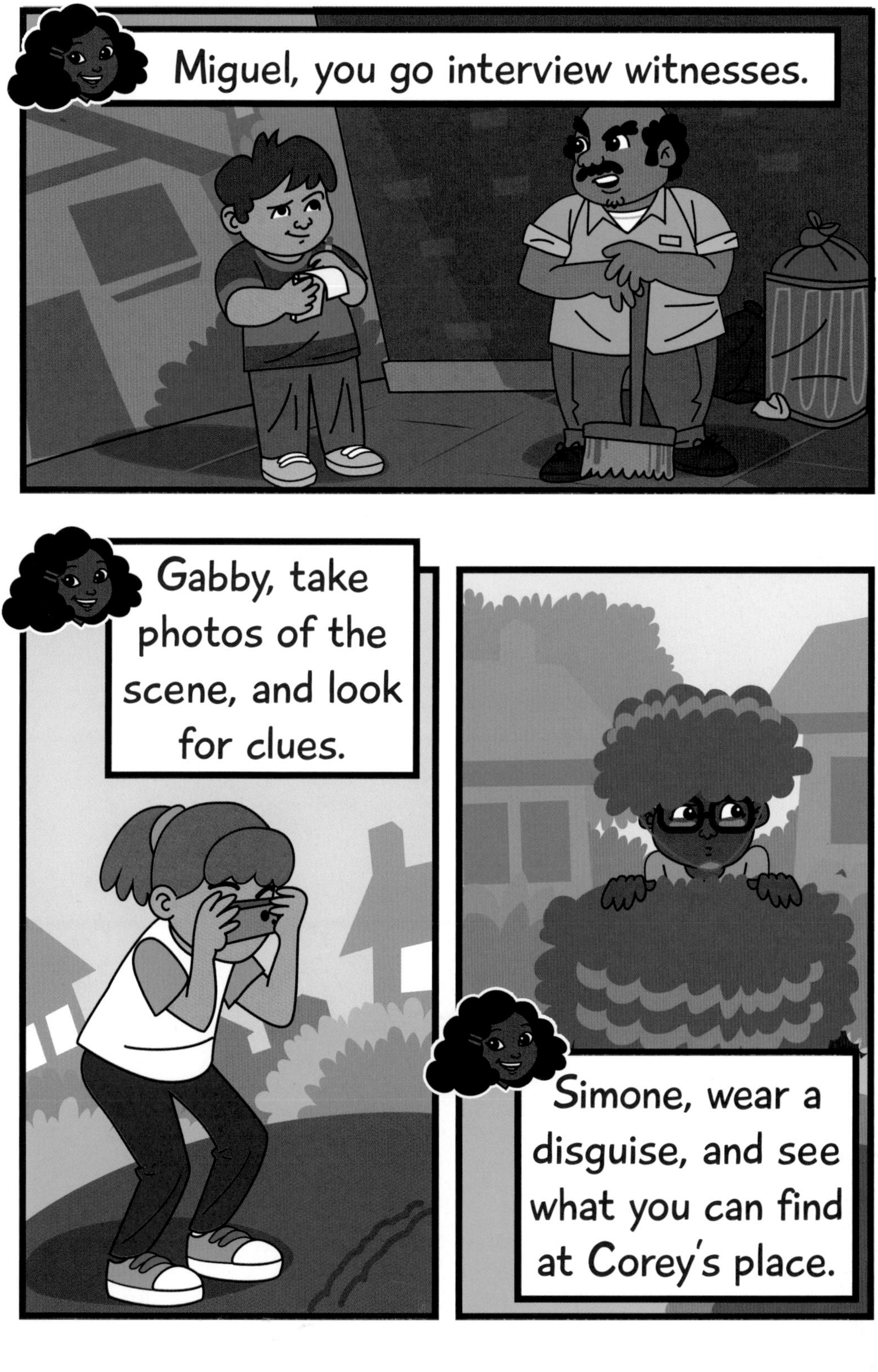
Miguel, you go interview witnesses.
Gabby, take photos of the scene, and look for clues.
Simone, wear a disguise, and see what you can find at Corey's place.

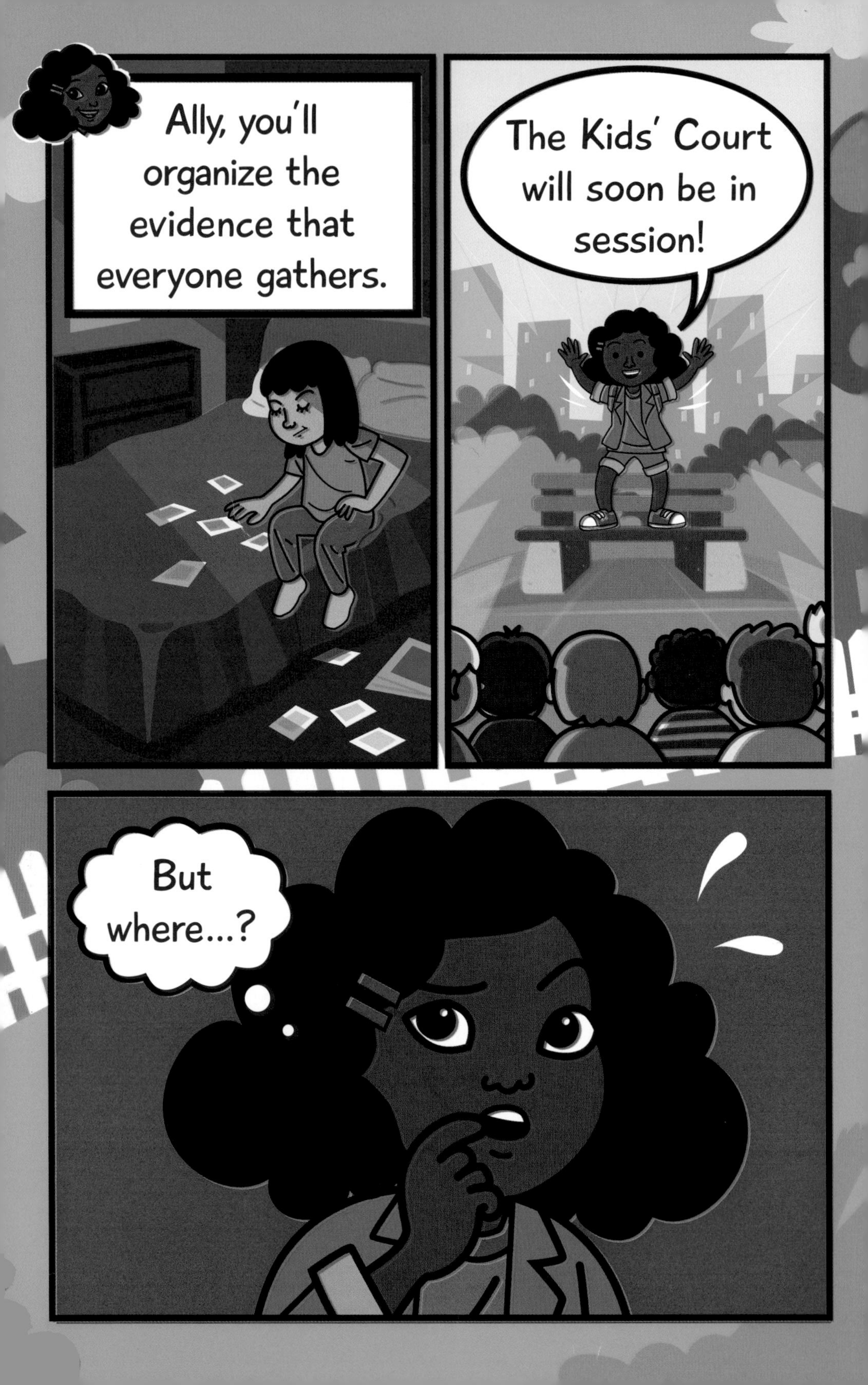
Ally, you'll organize the evidence that everyone gathers.
The Kids' Court will soon be in session!
But where...?

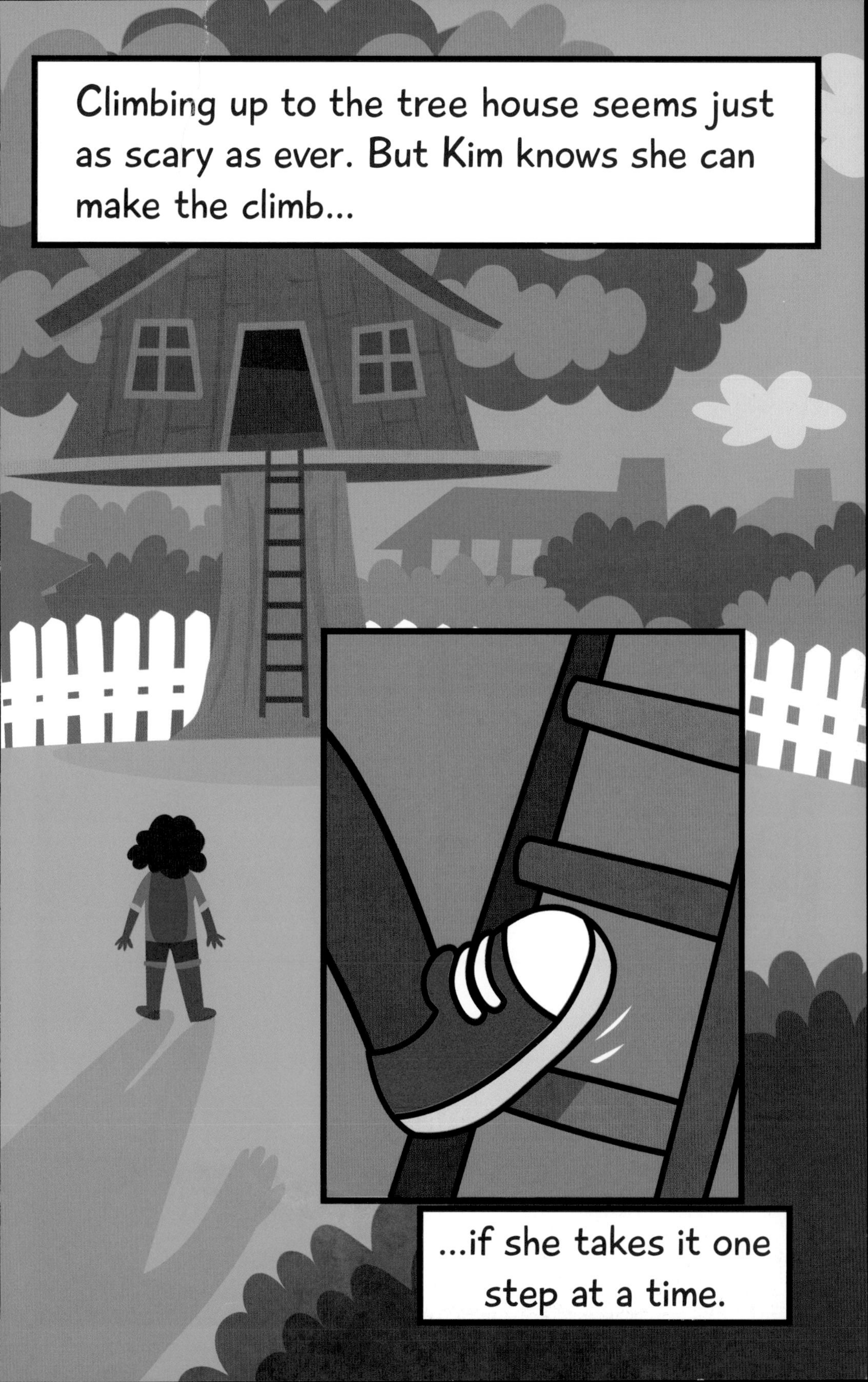
Climbing up to the tree house seems just as scary as ever. But Kim knows she can make the climb...
...if she takes it one step at a time.

Up the ladder Kim goes, never looking down.

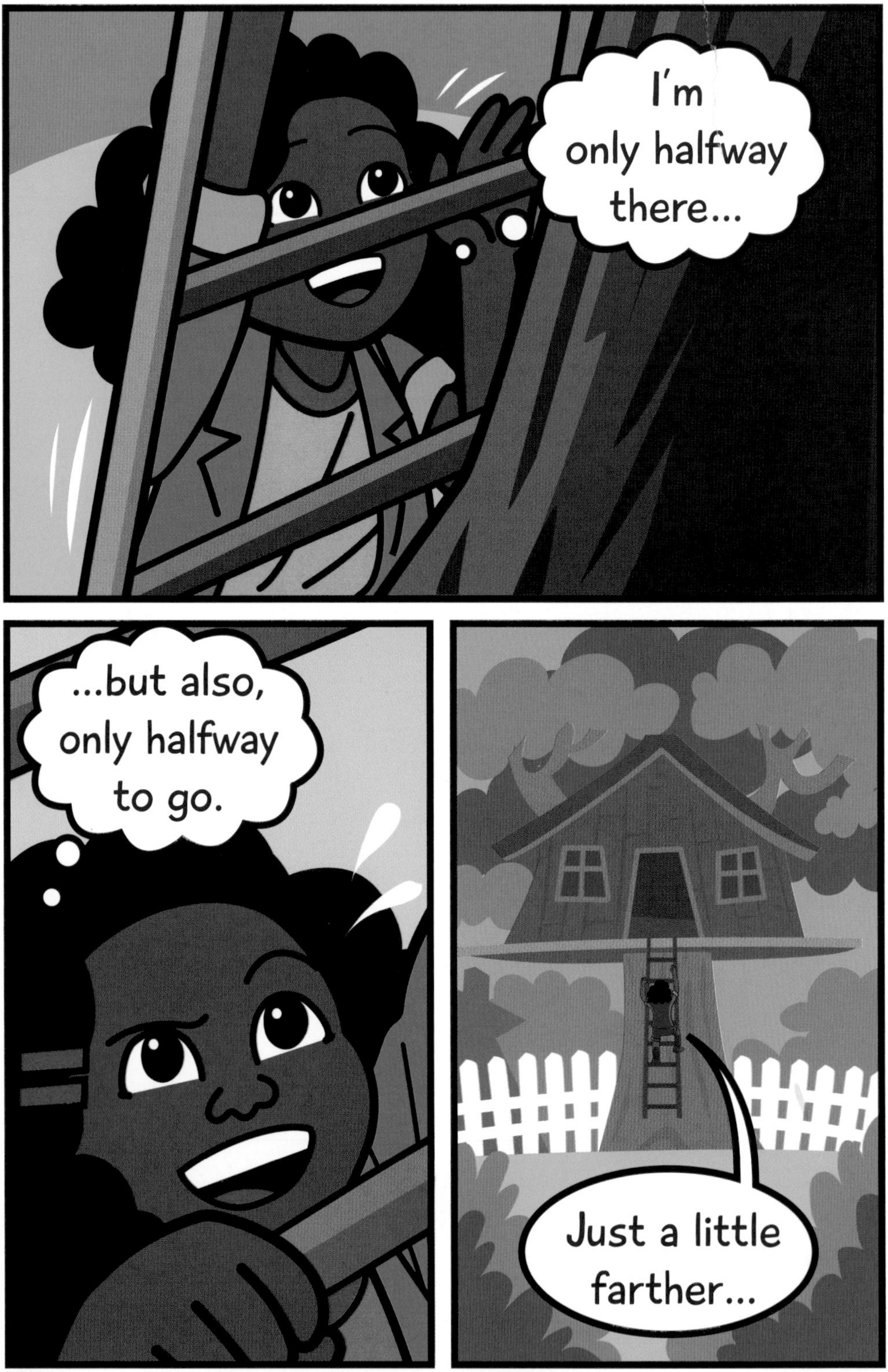
I'm only halfway there...
...but also, only halfway to go.
Just a little farther...

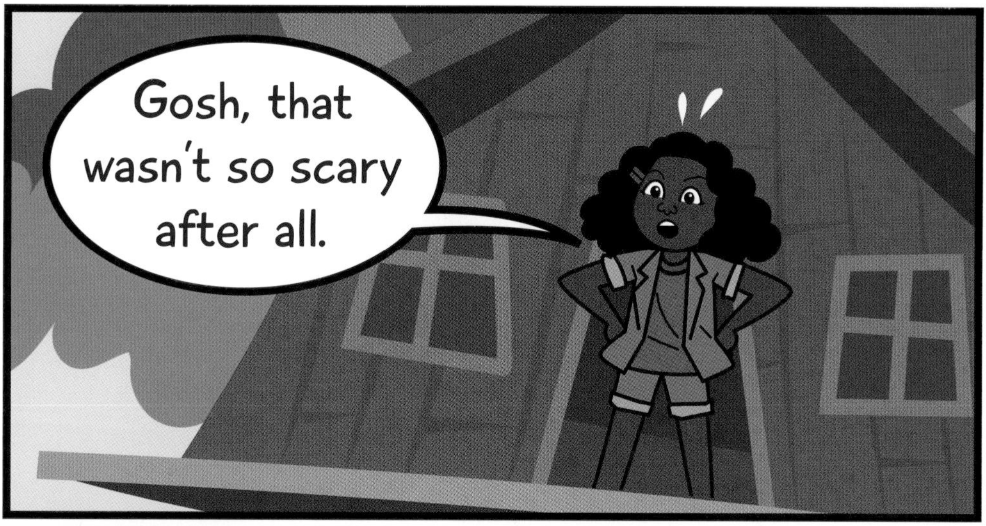
Gosh, that wasn't so scary after all.
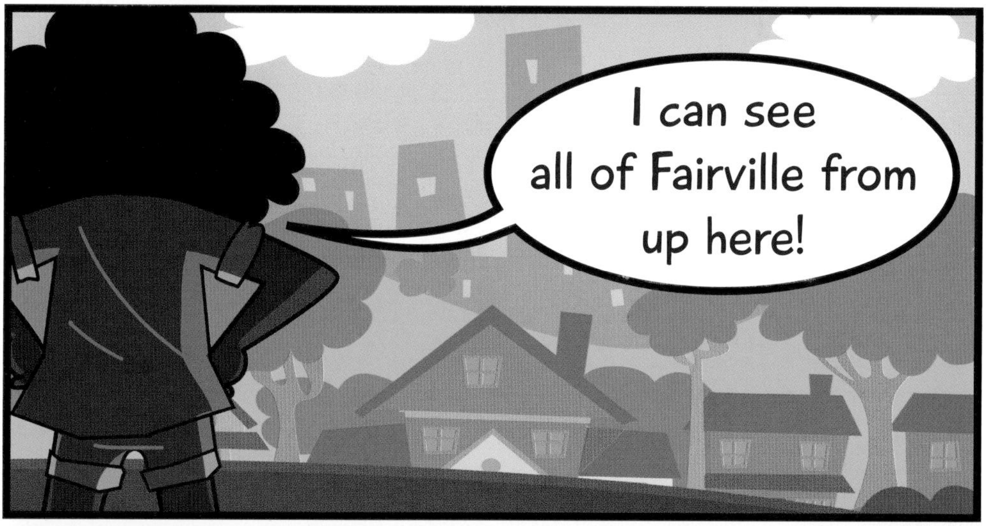
I can see all of Fairville from up here!
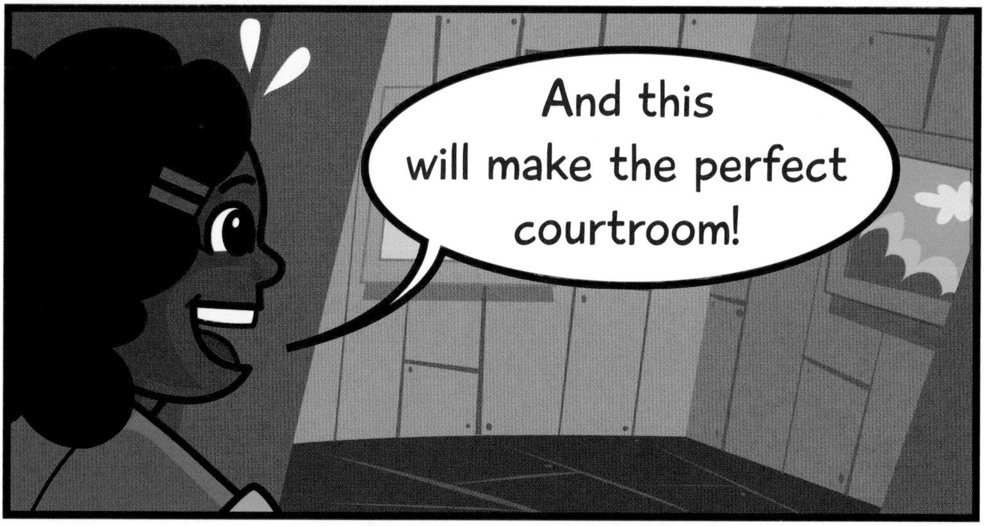
And this will make the perfect courtroom!

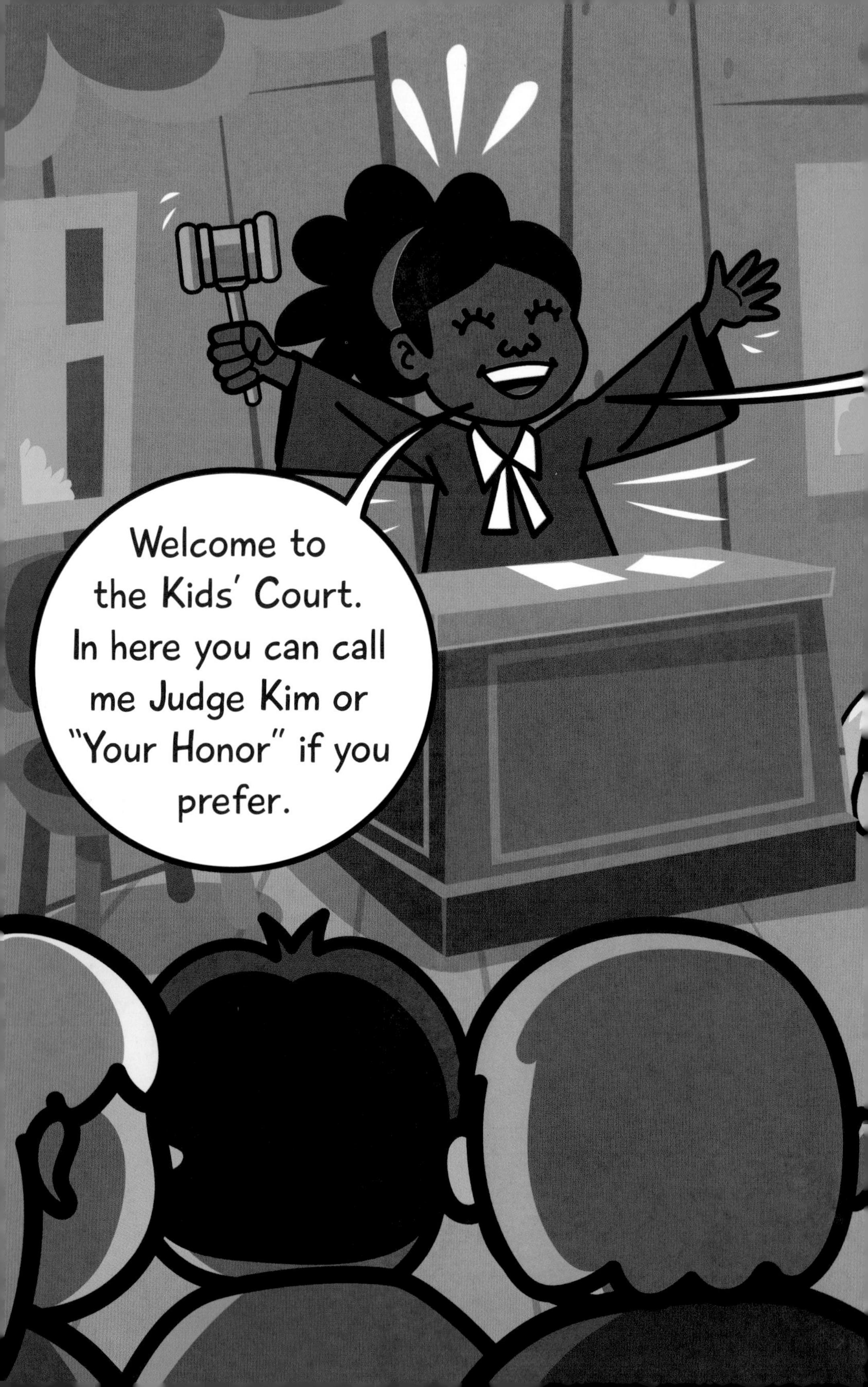
Welcome to the Kids' Court. In here you can call me Judge Kim or "Your Honor" if you prefer.

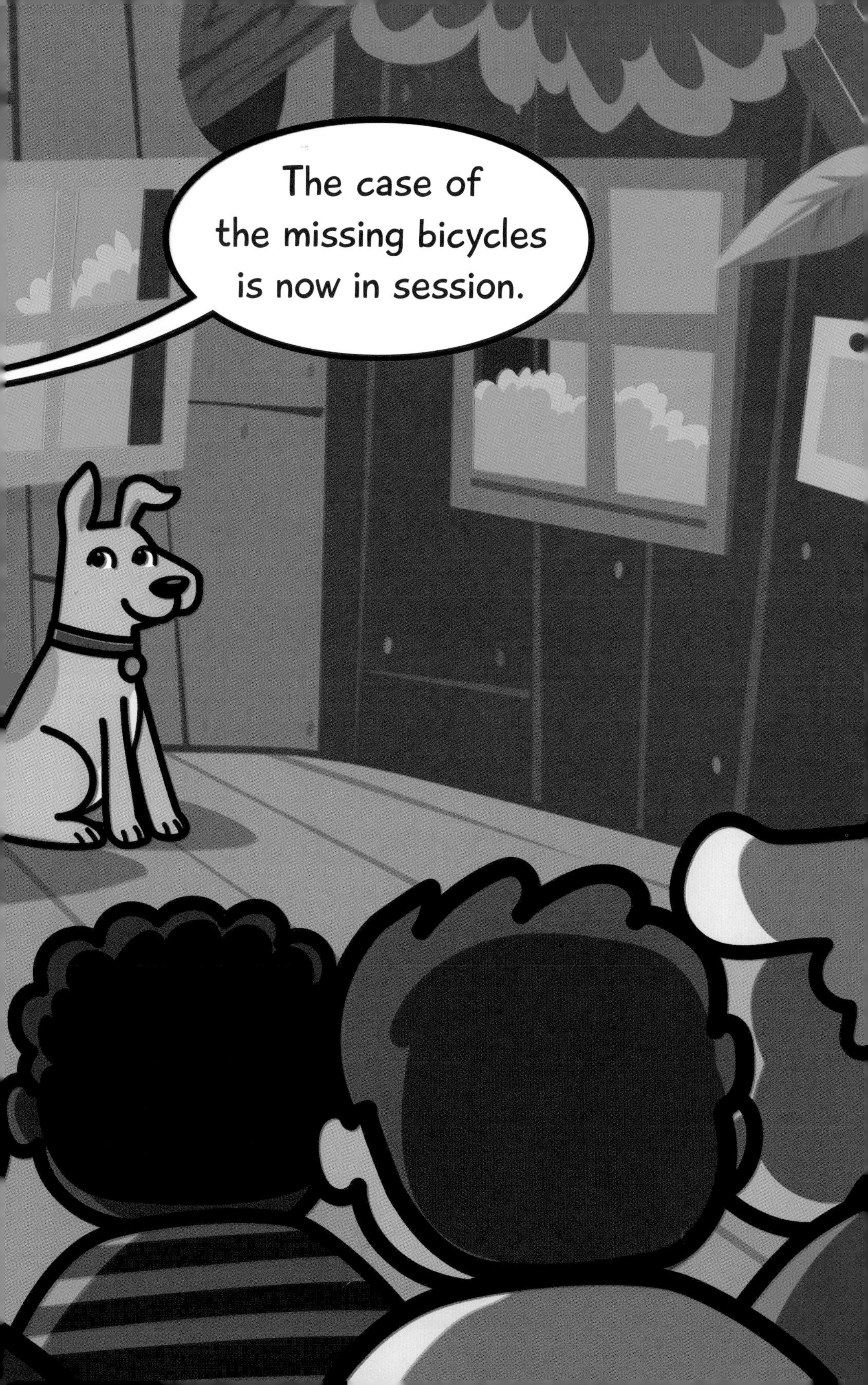
The case of the missing bicycles is now in session.

One by one the kids all get a chance to speak.

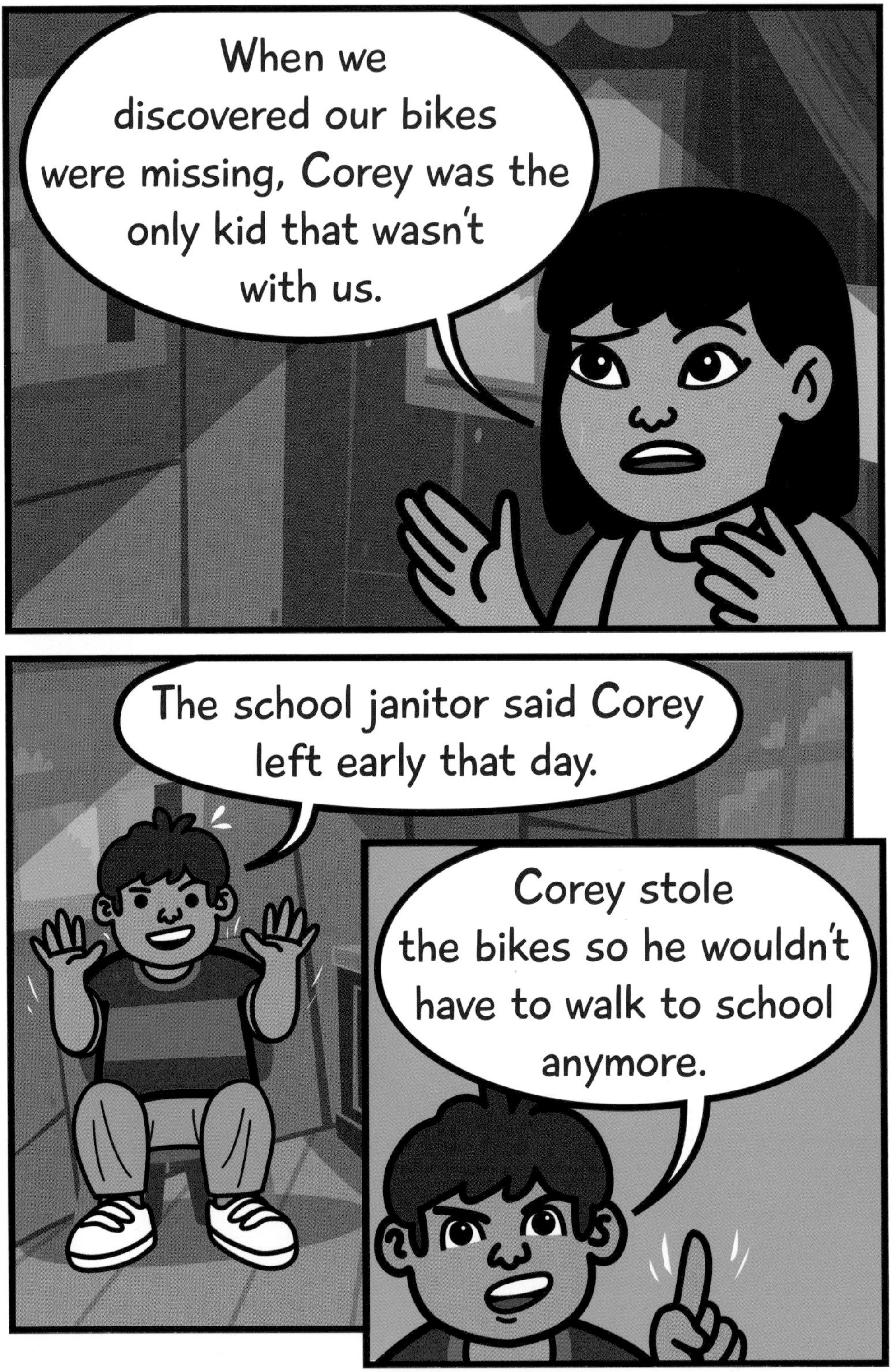
When we discovered our bikes were missing, Corey was the only kid that wasn't with us.
The school janitor said Corey left early that day.
Corey stole the bikes so he wouldn't have to walk to school anymore.

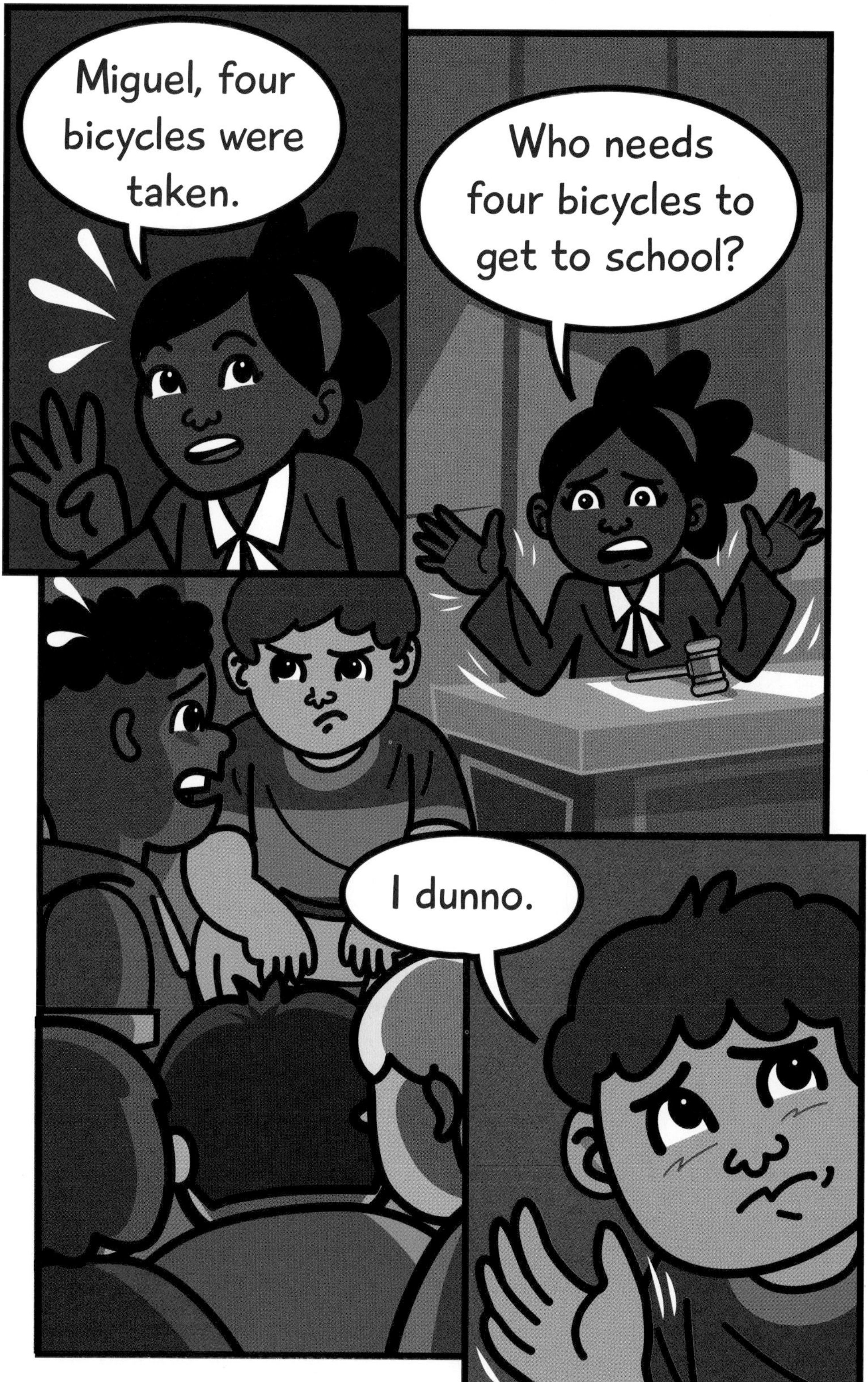
Miguel, four bicycles were taken.
Who needs four bicycles to get to school?
I dunno.

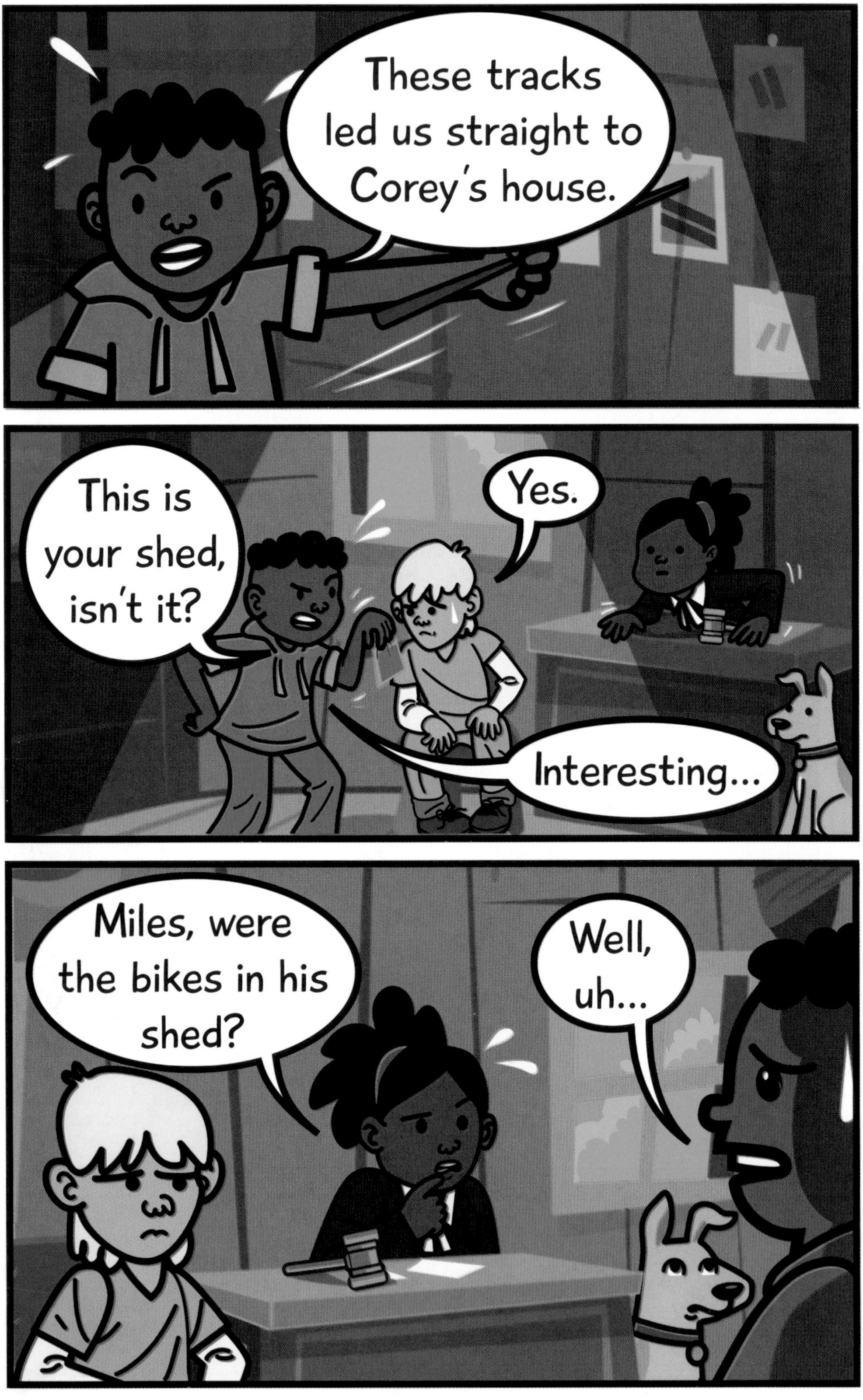
These tracks led us straight to Corey's house.
This is your shed, isn't it?
Yes.
Interesting...
Miles, were the bikes in his shed?
Well, uh...

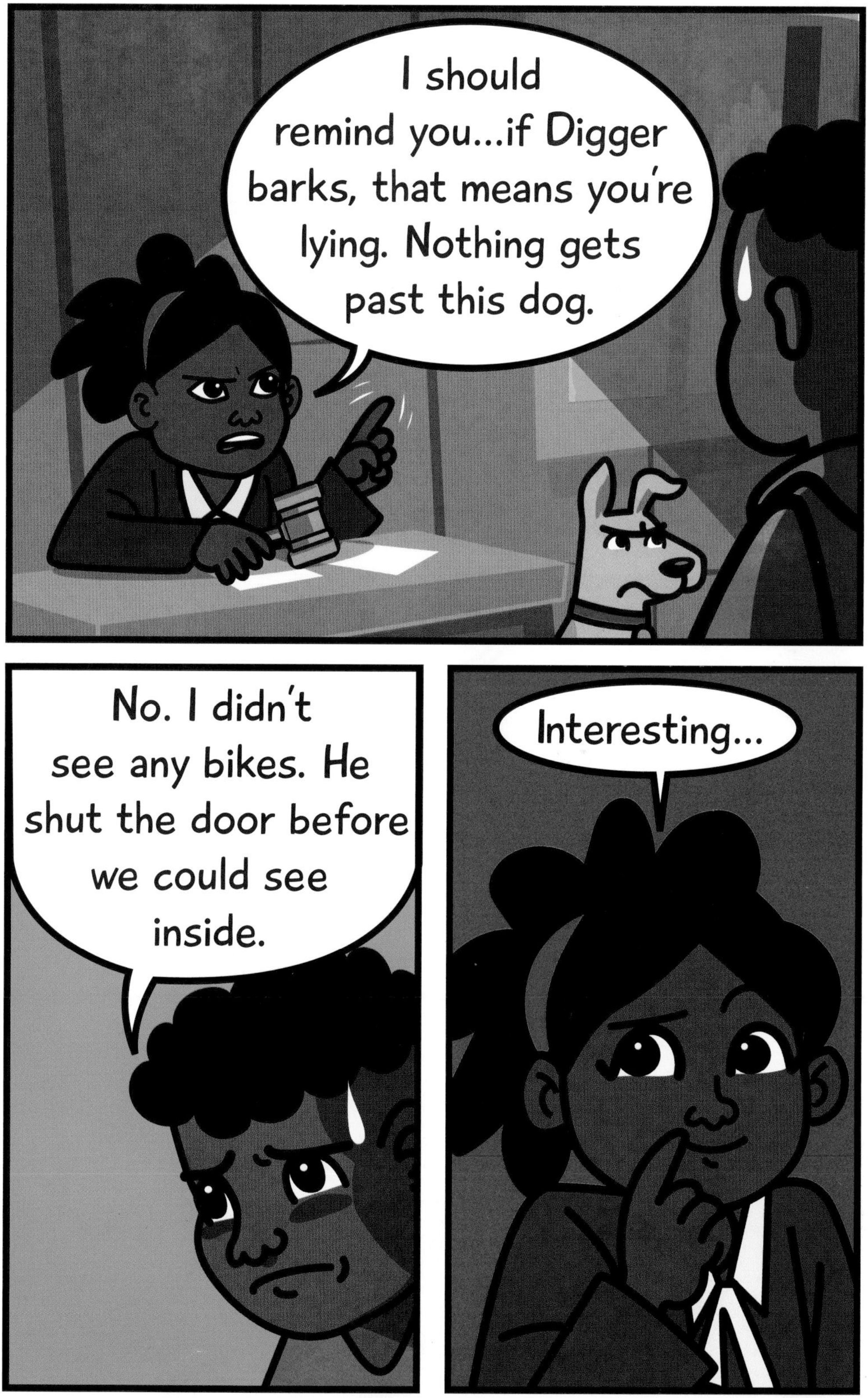
I should remind you...if Digger barks, that means you're lying. Nothing gets past this dog.
No. I didn't see any bikes. He shut the door before we could see inside.
Interesting...

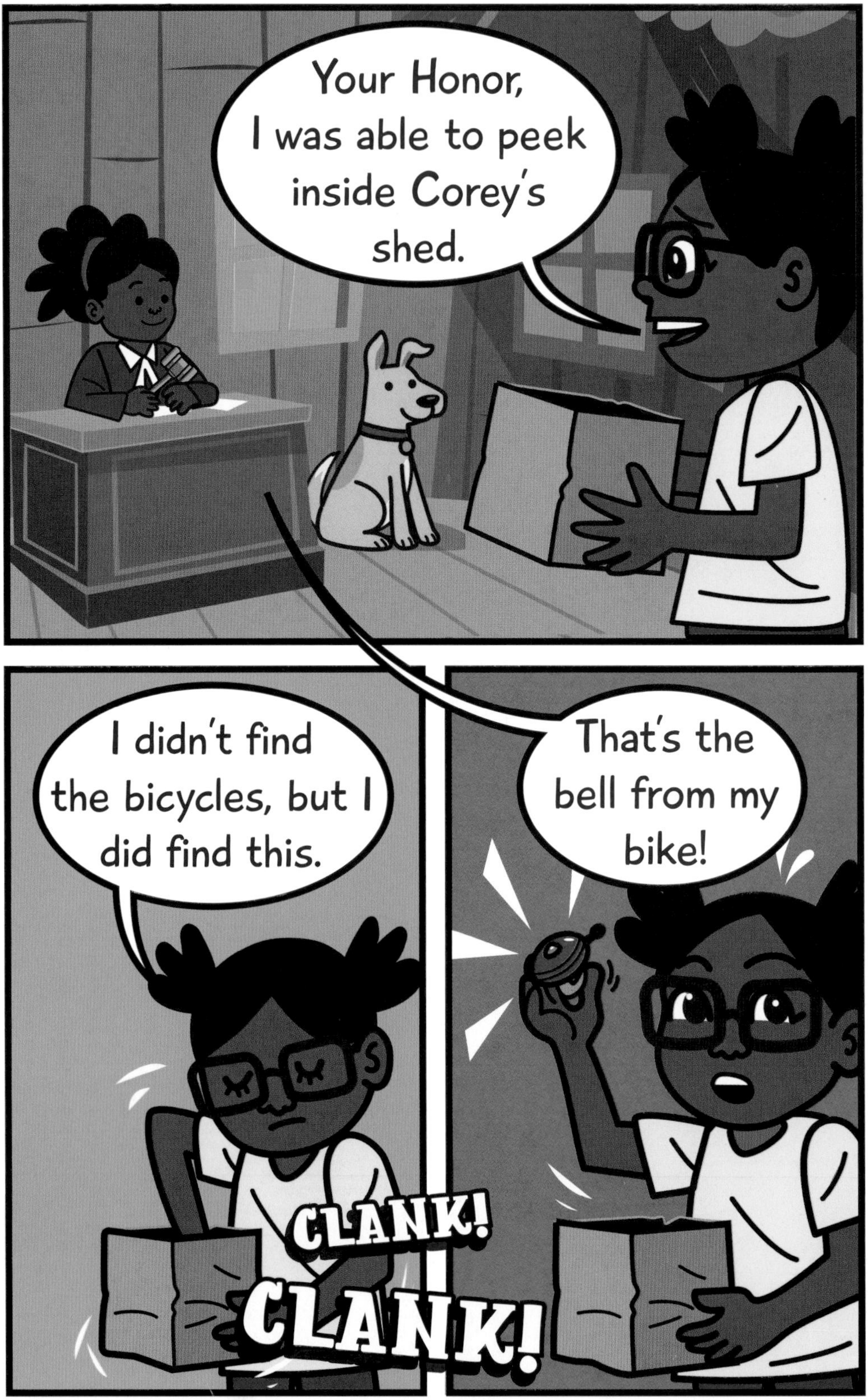
Your Honor, I was able to peek inside Corey's shed.
I didn't find the bicycles, but I did find this.
That's the bell from my bike!
CLANK!
CLANK!

Things aren't looking good for Corey.
The evidence against him is piling up.

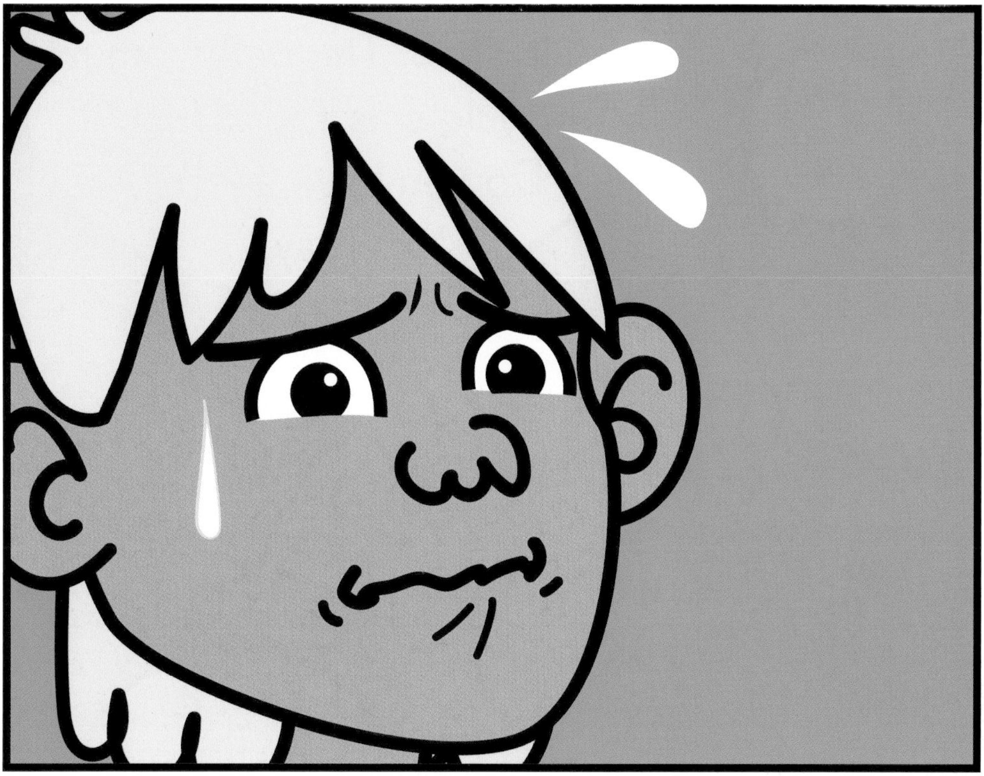

However, Kim knows that Corey deserves a chance to defend himself before she decides on the case.

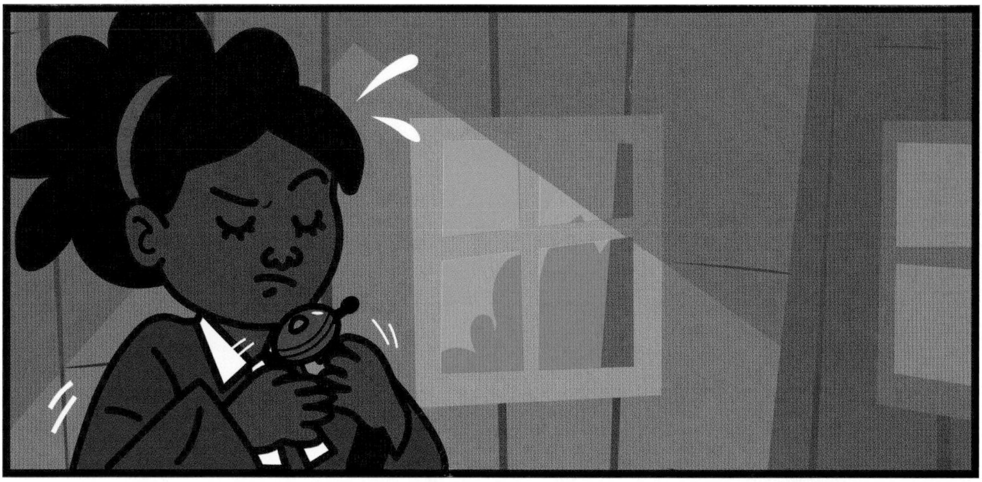

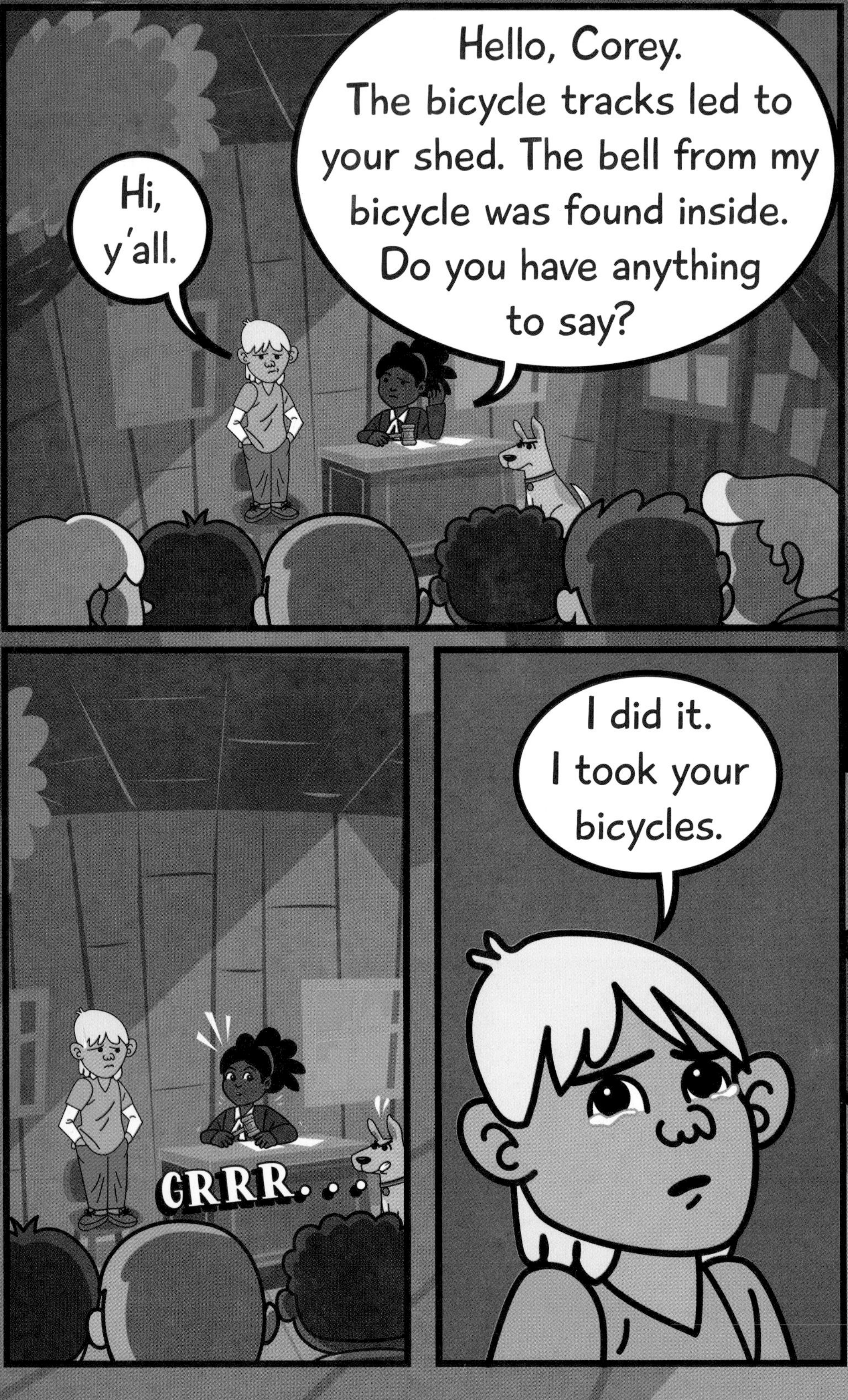
Hi, y'all.
Hello, Corey. The bicycle tracks led to your shed. The bell from my bicycle was found inside. Do you have anything to say?
GRRR. . .
I did it. I took your bicycles.

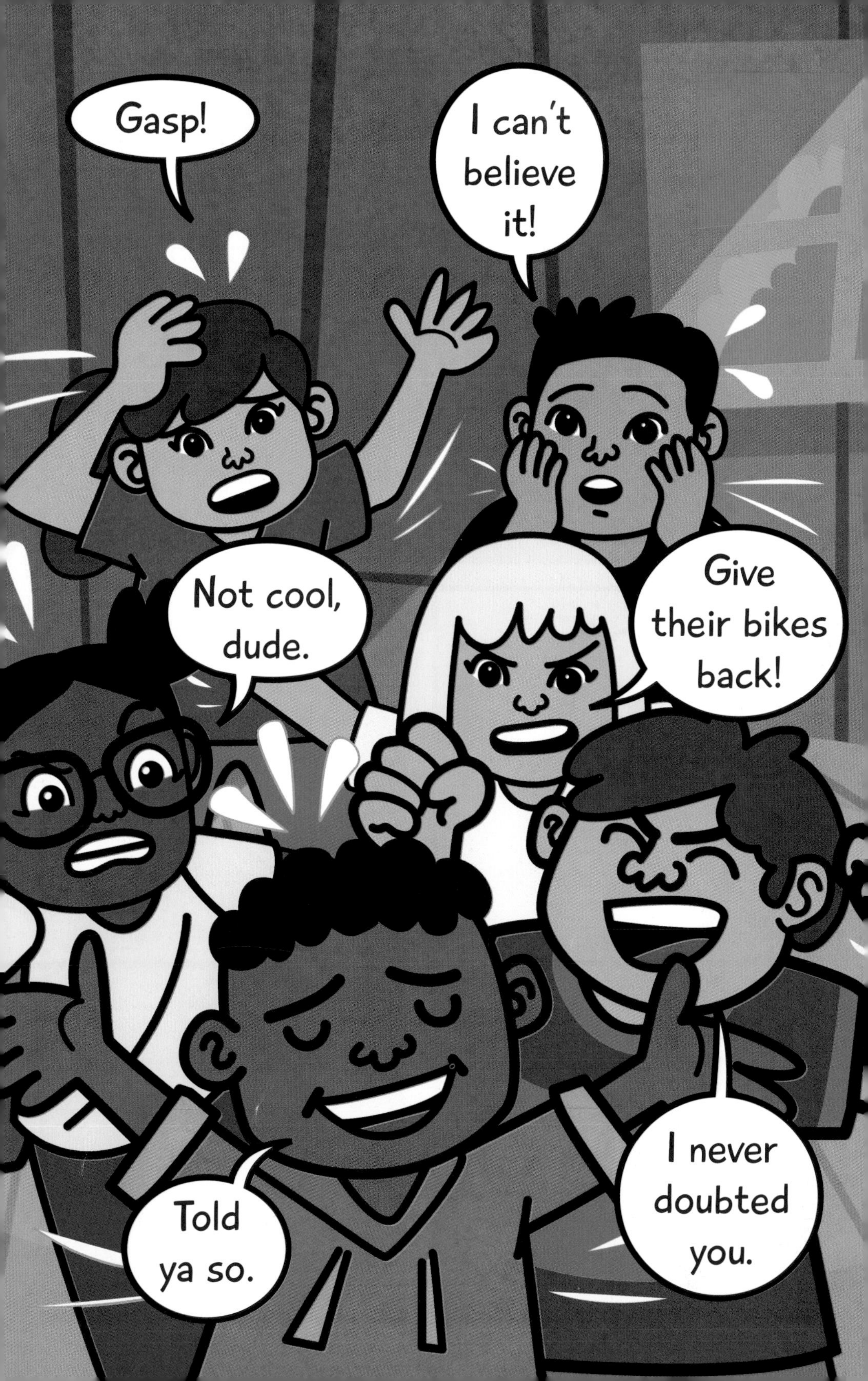
Gasp!
I can't believe it!
Not cool, dude.
Give their bikes back!
Told ya so.
I never doubted you.

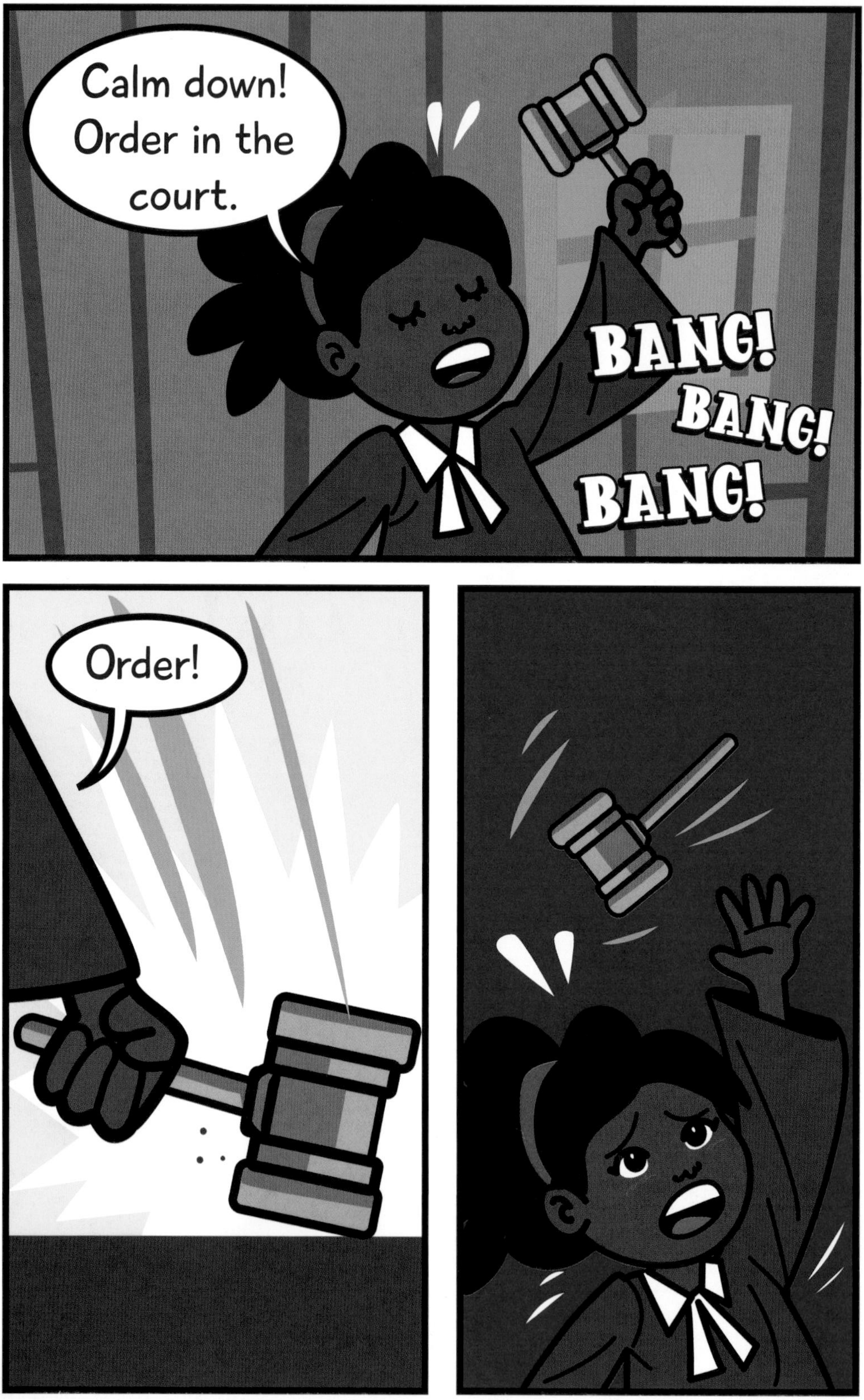
Calm down! Order in the court.
BANG!
BANG!
BANG!
Order!

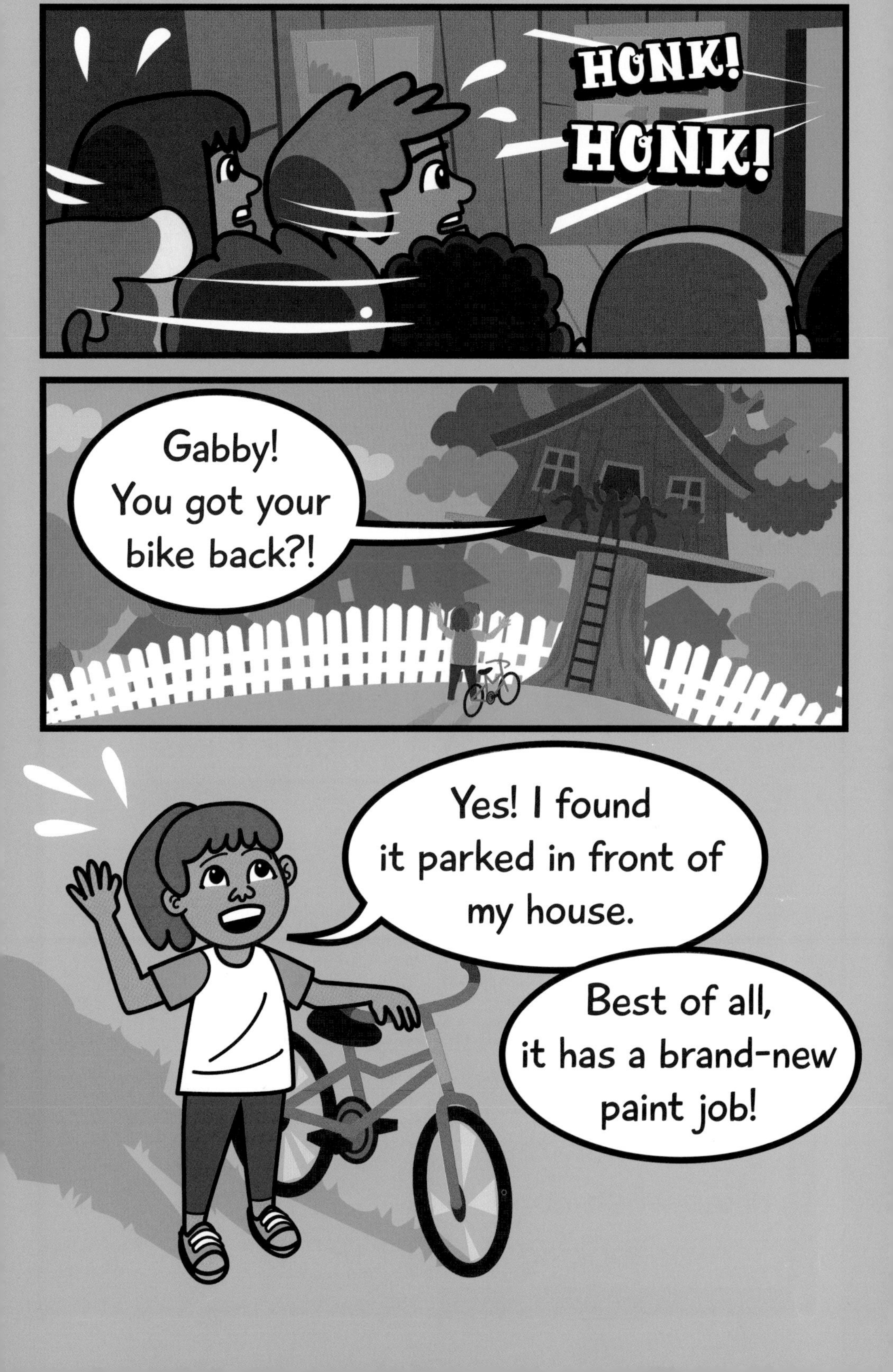
HONK!
HONK!
Gabby! You got your bike back?!
Yes! I found it parked in front of my house.
Best of all, it has a brand-new paint job!

The kids gather back inside to hear Corey's explanation.

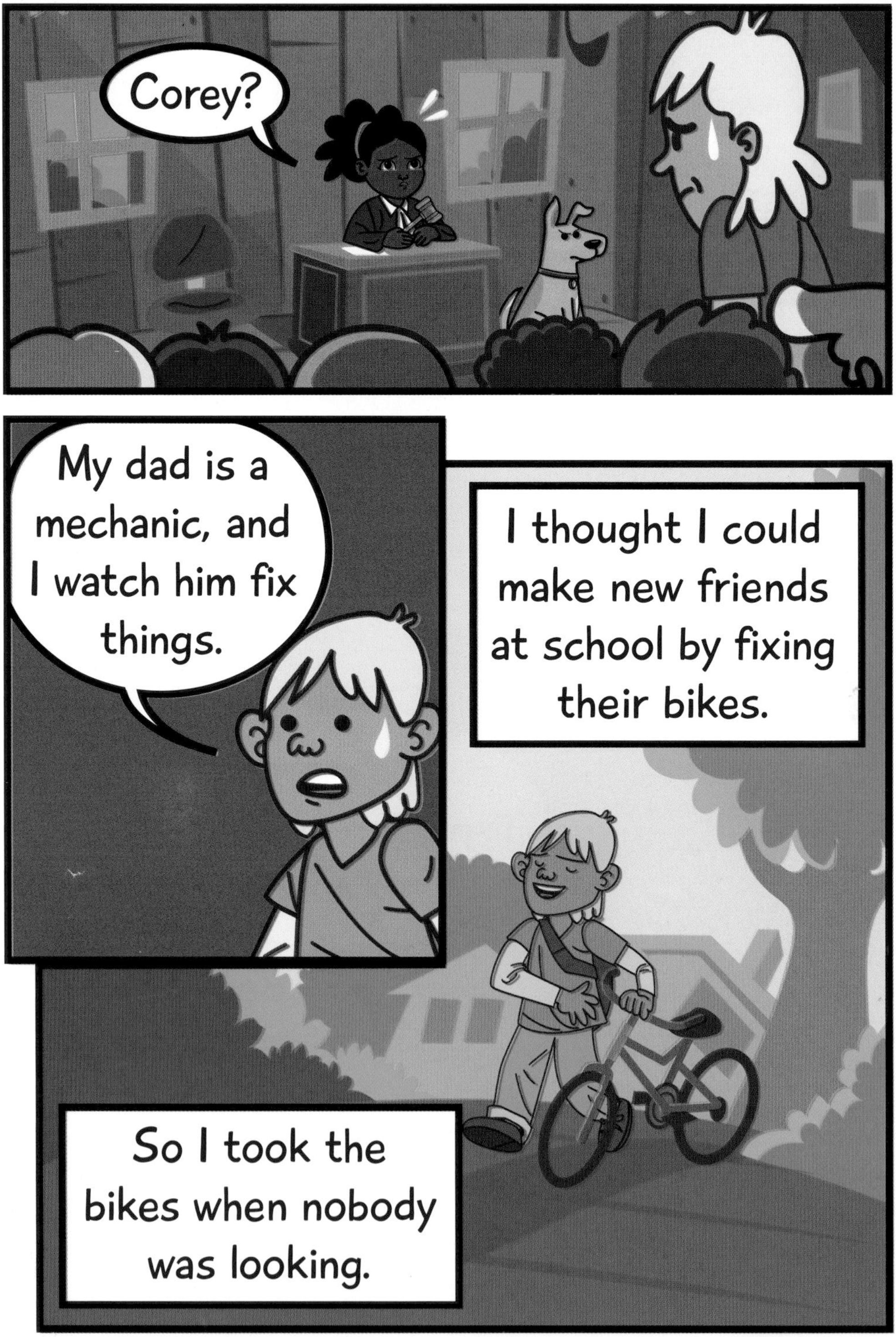
Corey?
My dad is a mechanic, and I watch him fix things.
I thought I could make new friends at school by fixing their bikes.
So I took the bikes when nobody was looking.

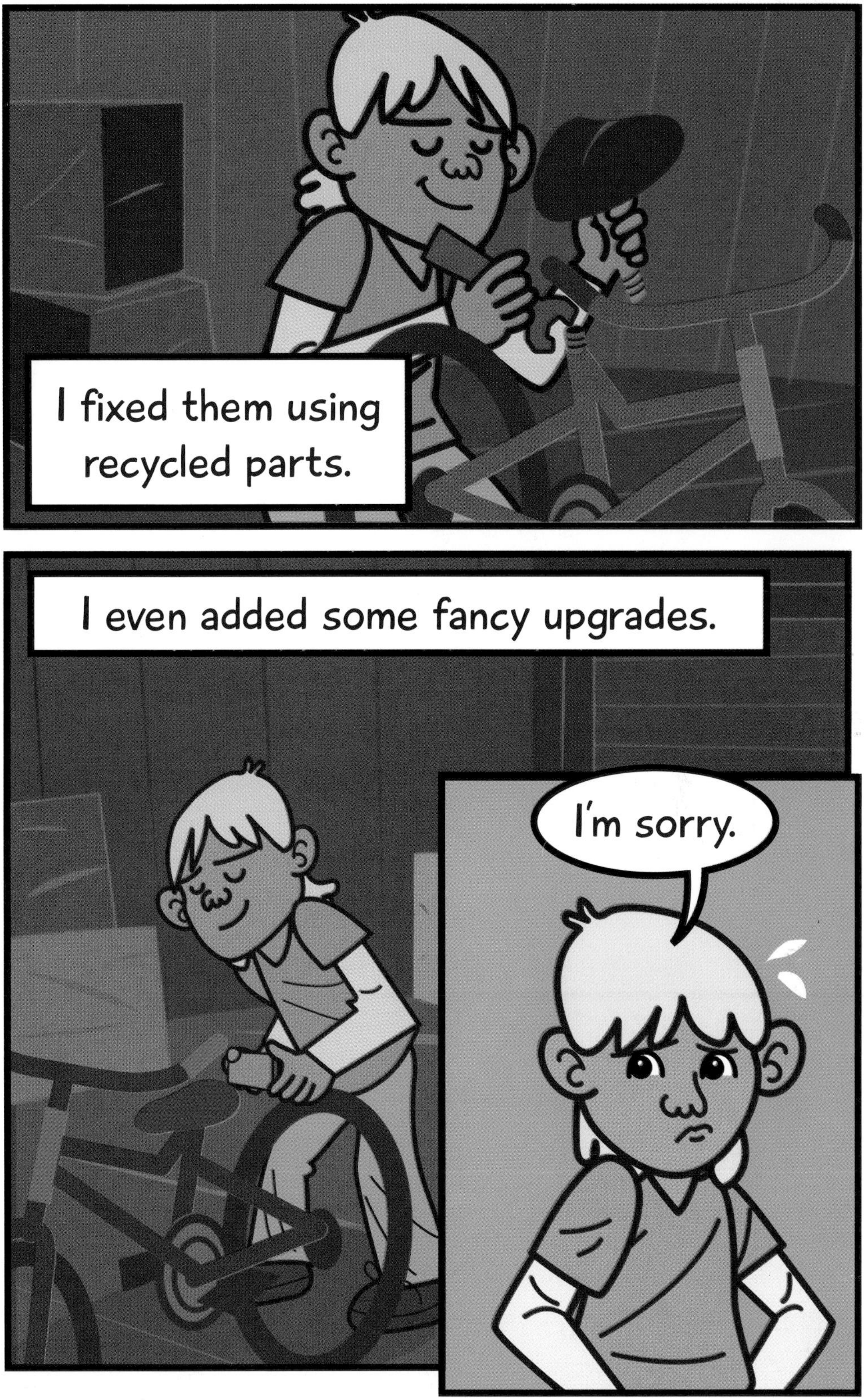
I fixed them using recycled parts.
I even added some fancy upgrades.
I'm sorry.

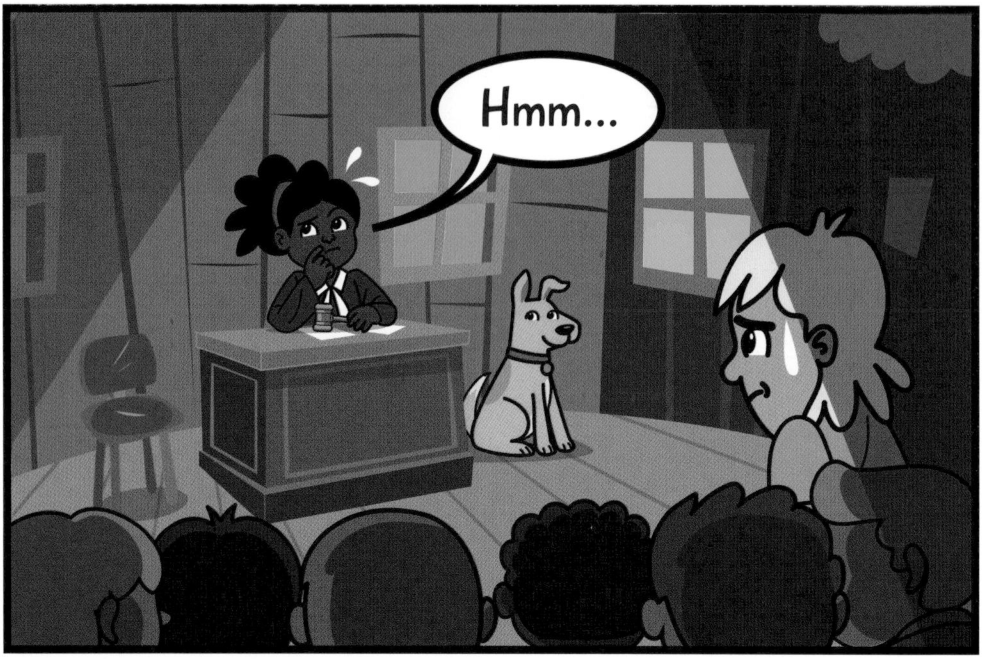
Hmm...

Kim thinks about everything that was presented. Now it's time for her to decide, who was right, and who was wrong?

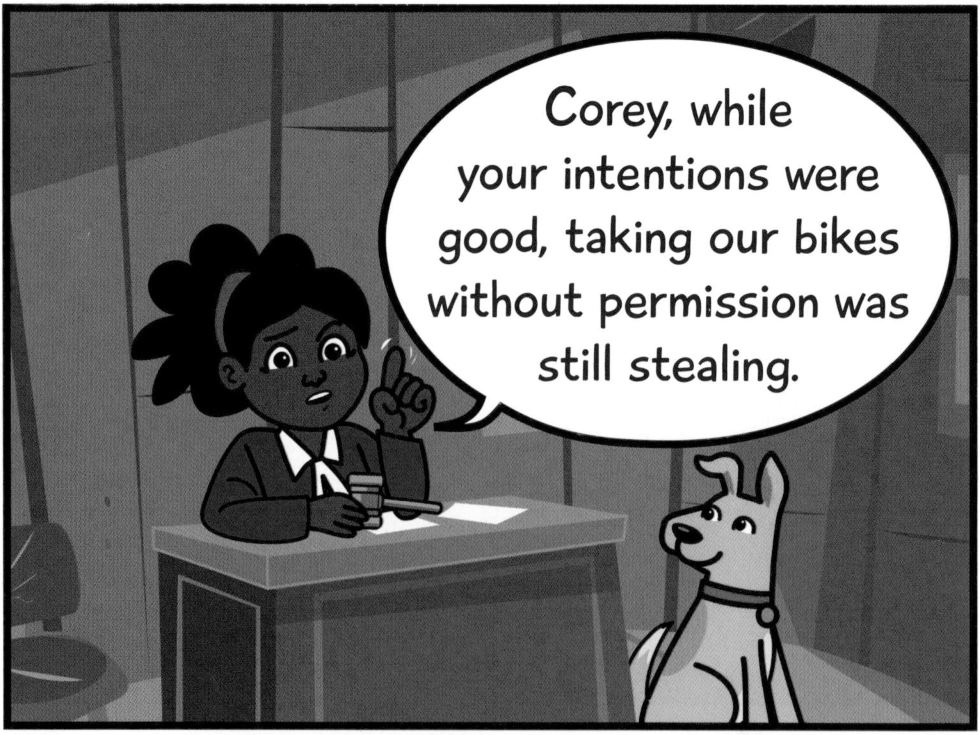
Corey, while your intentions were good, taking our bikes without permission was still stealing.

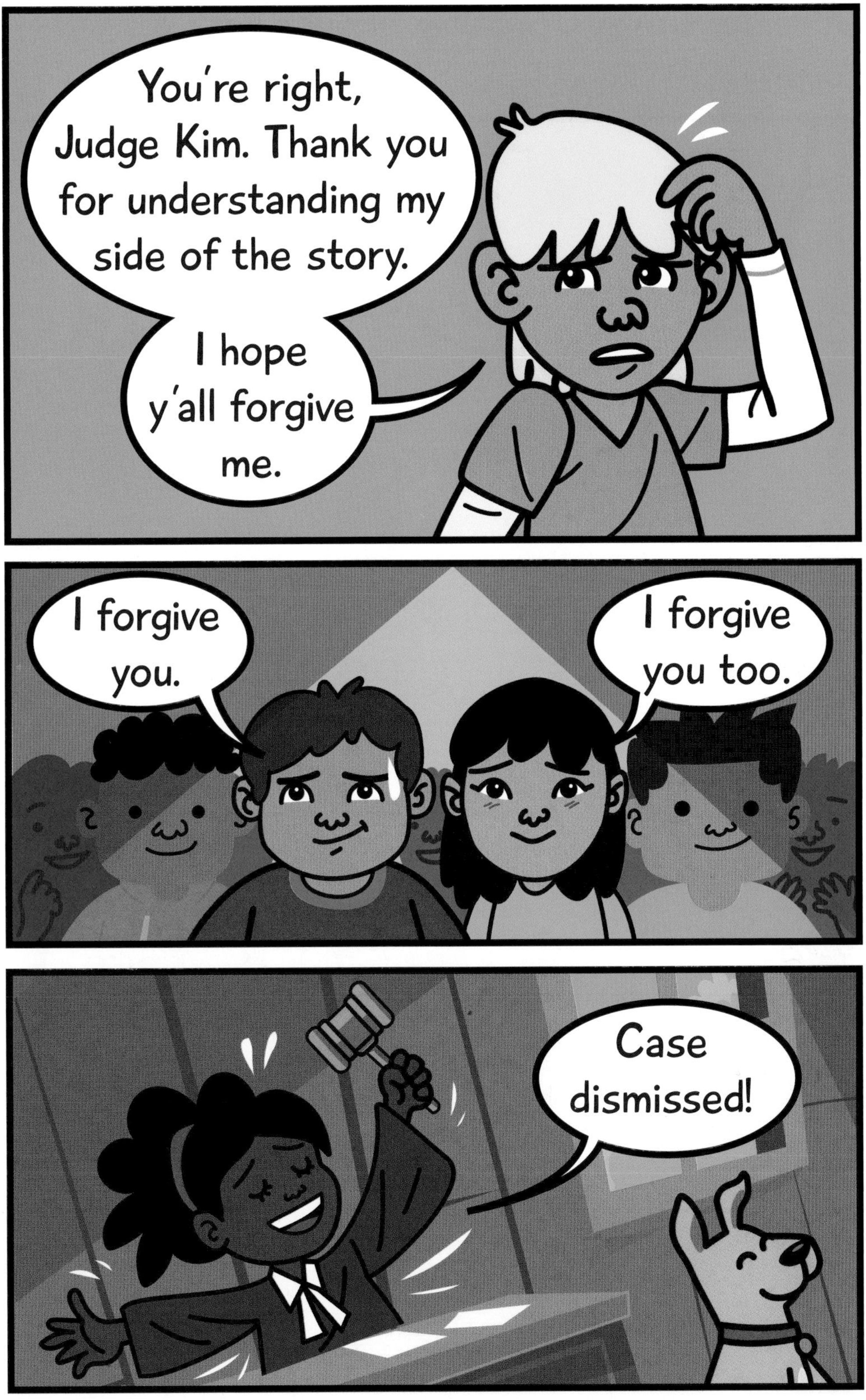
You're right, Judge Kim. Thank you for understanding my side of the story.
I hope y'all forgive me.
I forgive you.
I forgive you too.
Case dismissed!

Outside, Corey's brother arrives with a surprise.

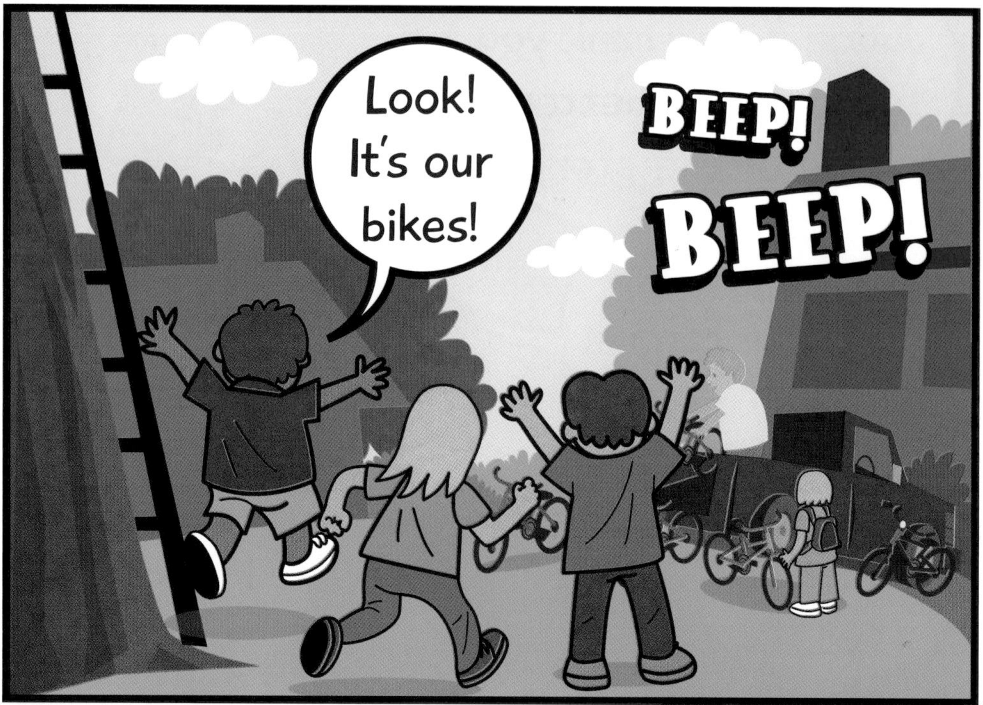
Look! It's our bikes!
BEEP!
BEEP!

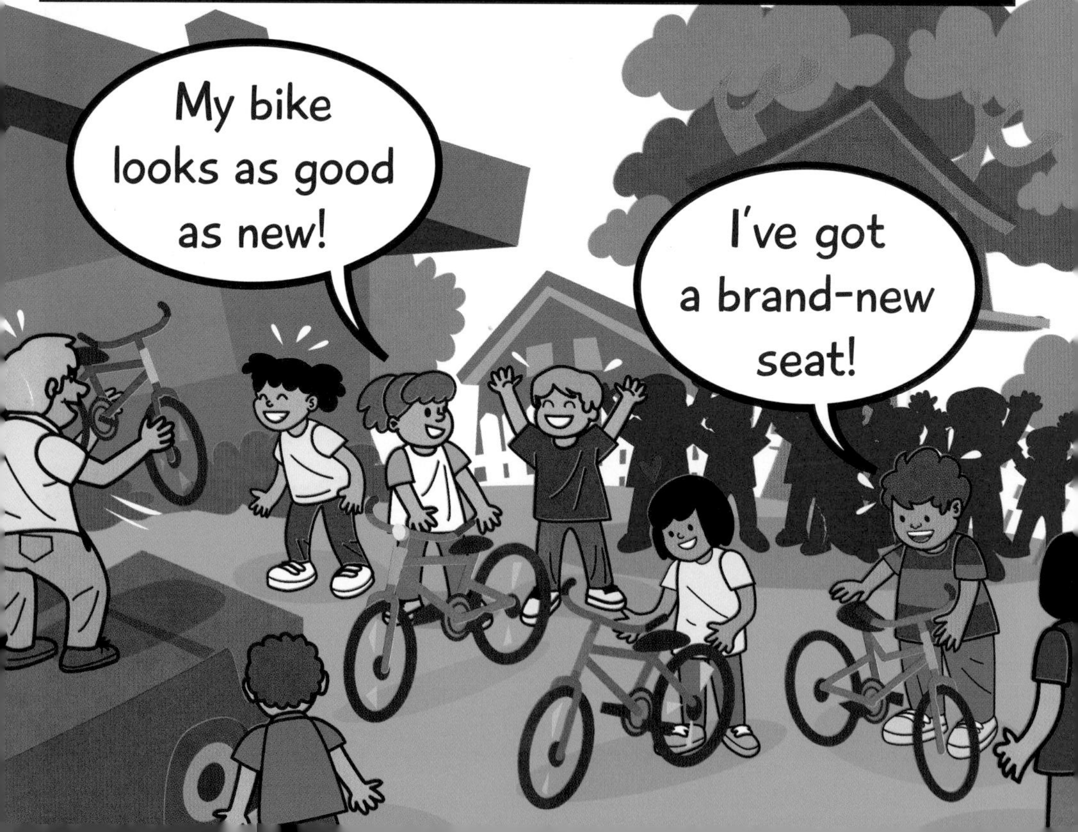
My bike looks as good as new!
I've got a brand-new seat!

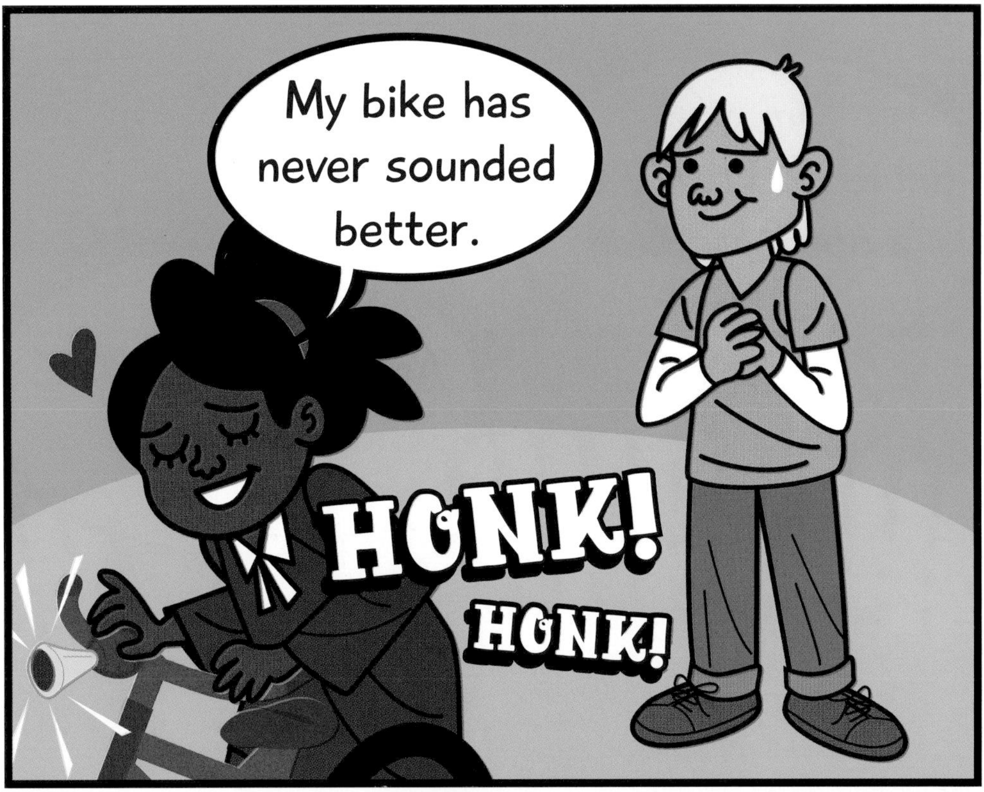
My bike has never sounded better.
HONK!
HONK!

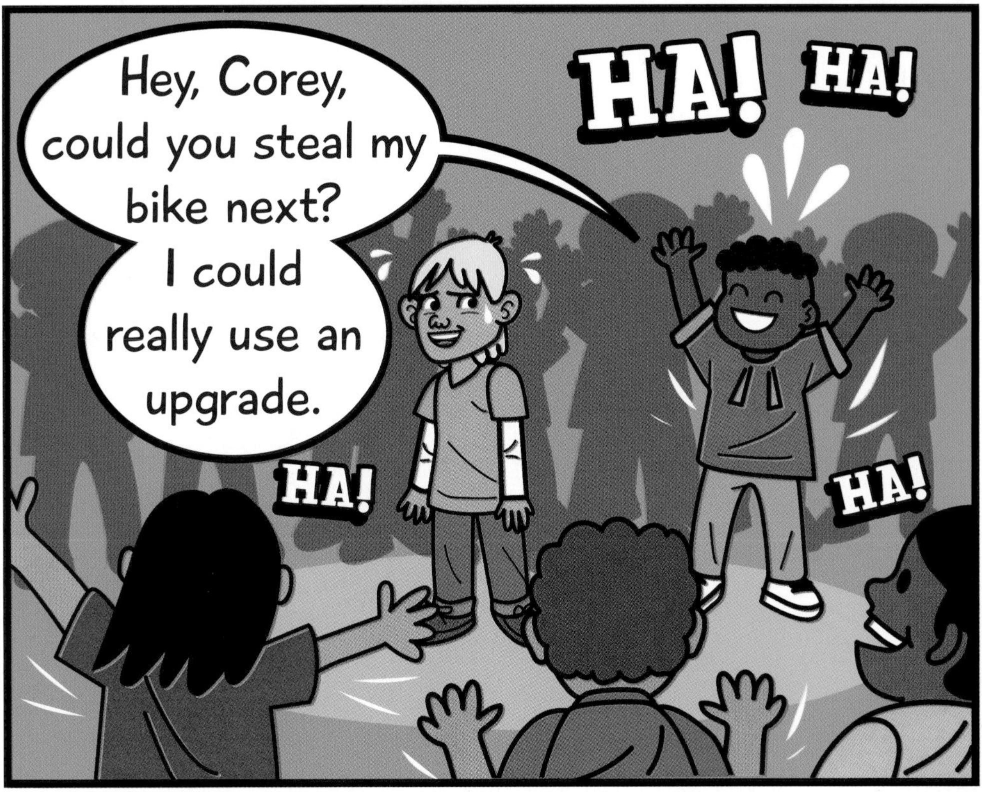
Hey, Corey, could you steal my bike next? I could really use an upgrade.
HA! HA!
HA!
HA!

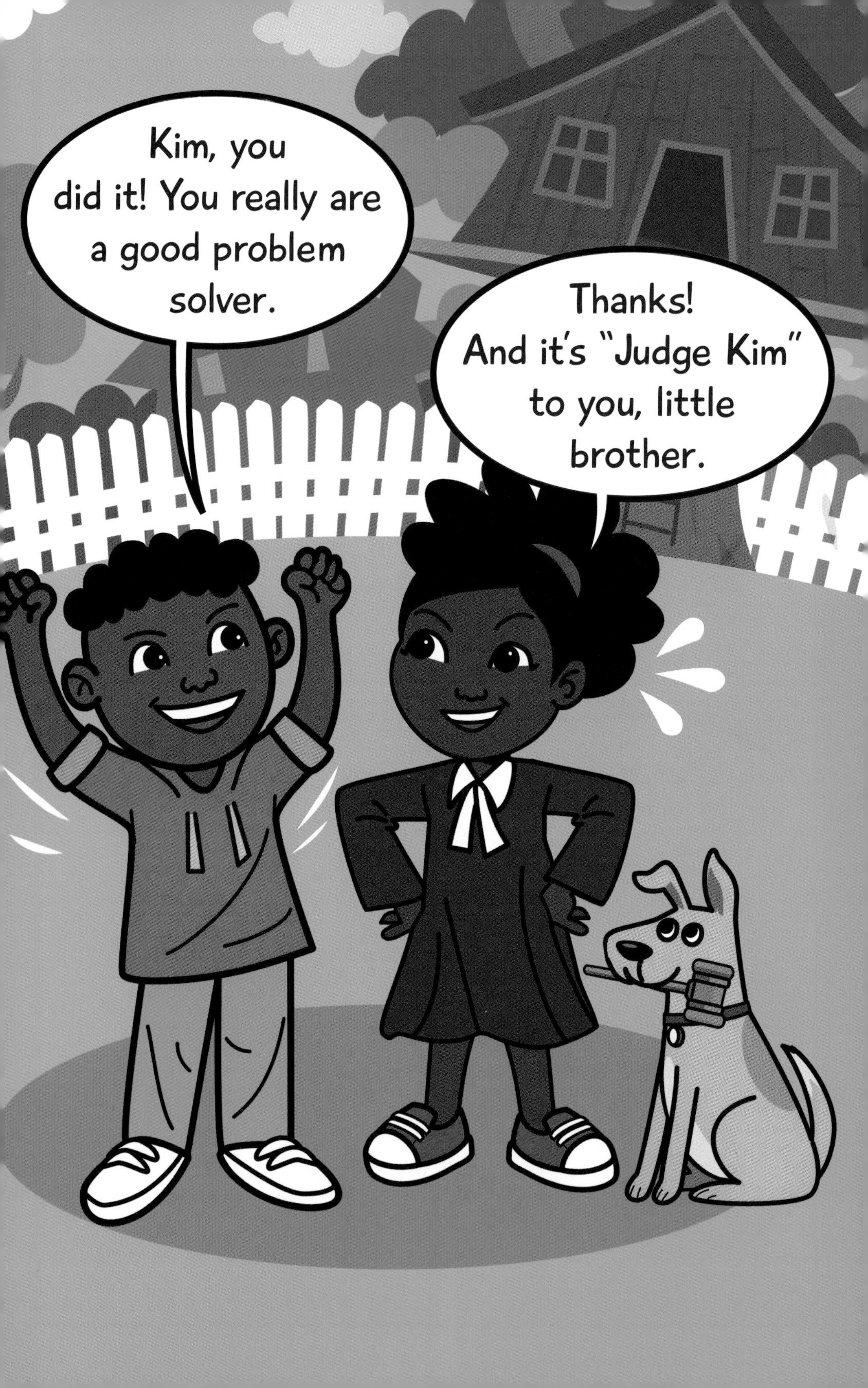
Kim, you did it! You really are a good problem solver.
Thanks! And it's "Judge Kim" to you, little brother.

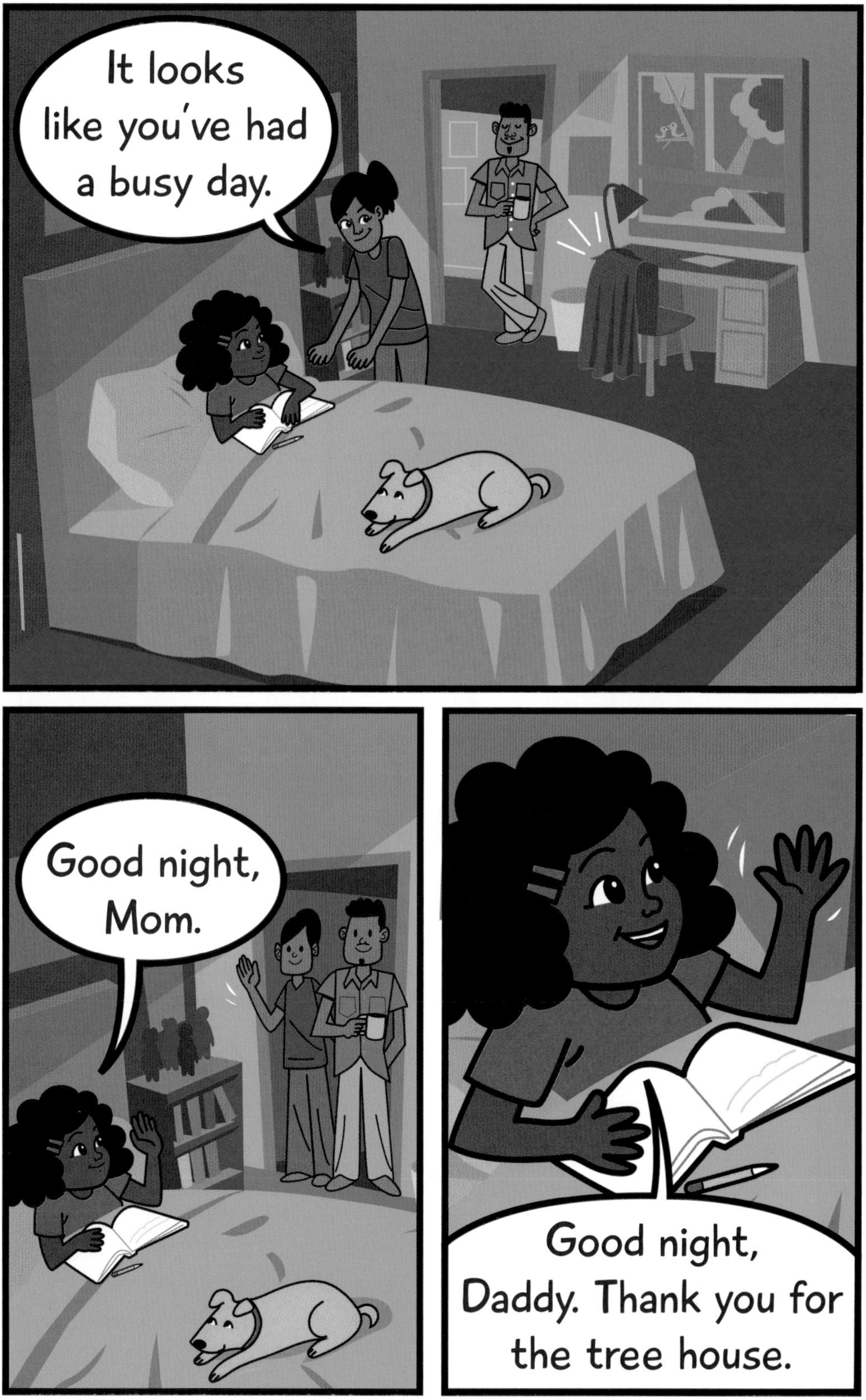
It looks like you've had a busy day.
Good night, Mom.
Good night, Daddy. Thank you for the tree house.

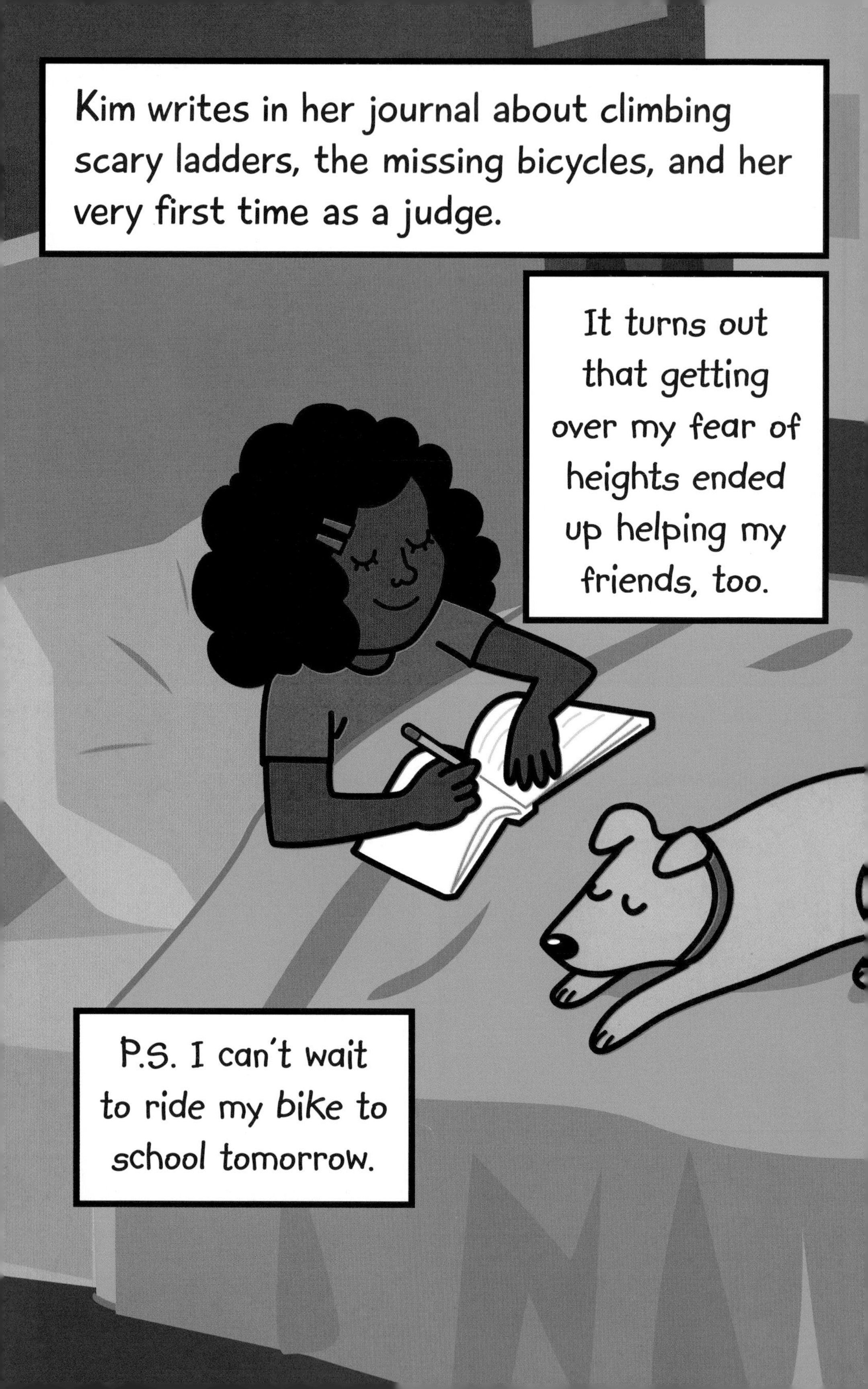
Kim writes in her journal about climbing scary ladders, the missing bicycles, and her very first time as a judge.
It turns out that getting over my fear of heights ended up helping my friends, too.
P.S. I can't wait to ride my *bike* to school tomorrow.

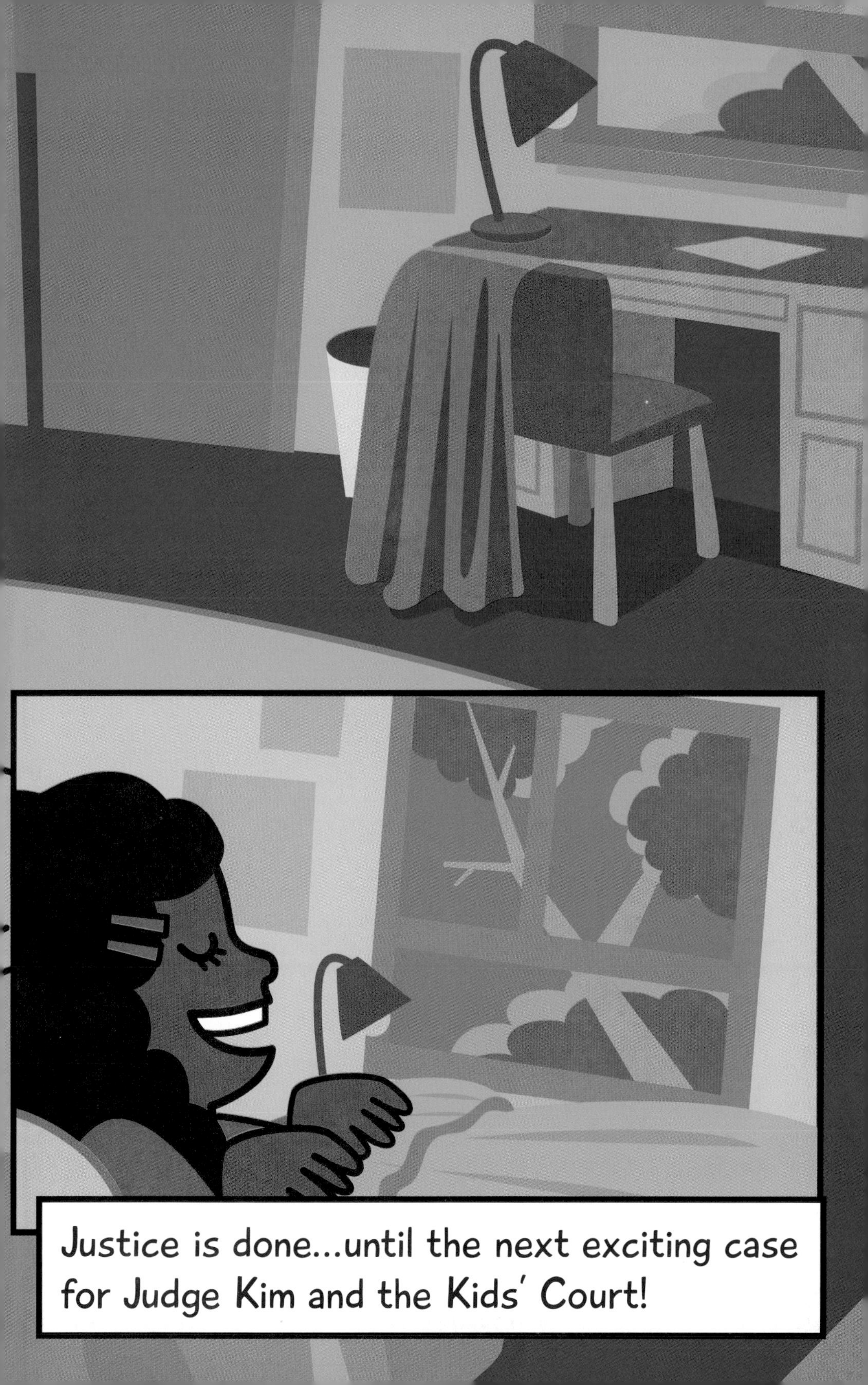
Justice is done...until the next exciting case for Judge Kim and the Kids' Court!

GLOSSARY

<u>case</u>: a disagreement between two people or groups that is decided in court.

<u>court</u>: a place where a judge listens to and decides on cases.

<u>evidence</u>: information presented in court to help a judge understand a case.

<u>judge</u>: a person who listens to cases and decides who is right and who is wrong.

<u>justice</u>: when a proper punishment or fair treatment is given by a judge.

<u>motive</u>: the reason a person did something or acted in a certain way.

<u>suspect</u>: a person who is believed to have done something wrong.

<u>witness</u>: a person who saw something happen that is related to a case.

Note to readers: Some of these words may have more than one definition. The definitions above match how these words are used in this book.